I Scream,
You Scream

A Willow Crier Cozy Mystery

Book 2

Lilly York

I Scream, You Scream

A Willow Crier Cozy Mystery

Book 2

©2015 by Lilly York

www.lillyyork.com

Cover Design: Jonna Feavel
40daygraphics.com

Illustrations: Ben Gerhards

Interior Layout: Daniel Mawhinney
40daypublishing.com

Published by: Wide Awake Books
wideawakebooks.com

Also available in eBook publication

Printed in the United States of America

Get your free short story!

Grandpa Goes Missing

Find out what happened to bring Willow down to Oklahoma in the first place.

FREE short story only available here!

www.lillyyork.com/shortstory

Get yours today!

Chapter 1

Willow loved listening to the whir of her new cappuccino machine. She finally invested in updating the Willow Tree Sweet Shoppe and part of that renovation was a brand new specialty coffee bar. She loved the new look. She tried to please all her customers, which was tough to do since trying to please everyone has always been futile and completely against Willow's nature. Her ice cream parlor was brightly lit with colorful candy hues. The other half of her shop was now a coffee bar and was muted and serene in earth tones. She had a glass wall built between the two dining areas to keep the coffee bar area quiet while the ice cream side was fun and playful. While the dining area was separated, the work area behind the counter was one long service area. Which meant any employee could take care of customers on both sides of the store. It was a big investment, but so far everyone seemed happy.

She had doubled her business since adding the coffee line. People would stop by the shop on their way to work, if they were meeting a friend, or if they just felt like a good cup of coffee to go with the book they were reading. She even had an author or two who came in regularly to write. She had no idea authors lived in her area of the world. She thought they all lived in New York or L.A. She tried to peek every now and again to see what they were working on, but she didn't want to lose their business so she tried not to be too nosy.

Today, her mystery writer was in. He pretty much kept to himself. He didn't divulge much, but once in a while he would throw out an idea and get her opinion on it. He loved her coffee and pastries. The comfortable working stations helped too.

She finished making his coffee. "Here you go, Mr. Rune." She handed him the coffee and took his fiver. They had it down to a science now. The change went into the tip jar which was split between all the employees at the end of the night.

Willow whispered his first name when he was out of range of hearing. Huxley Rune. Best-selling mystery author. New York Times Best Selling Author. She wondered if he had programmed Siri on his phone to say, "Hello New York Times Best Selling Author" when she was addressing him. She would if she was a best-selling author.

She looked at her watch. She still had a few things to do for the ice cream festival that was kicking off the next afternoon. Including getting her shop ready for the Karaoke party which started in less than two hours.

Mr. Rune would be taking his computer and leaving for the night when he realized what would be going on. Karaoke. The town loved it. He hated it.

Her glass partition wall was on a track and could be opened to make one big room for bigger parties. It was fantastic. She had so many options with this new system.

The guy she hired to run karaoke walked through the door and she waved him over. She had a little stage in the coffee shop side, which she used for open mic night as well as karaoke.

"Hey, Mitch, what would you like to drink?"

He perused the menu. "Hmm, how about a bigger Frappuccino?"

"Okay, I'll get it ready for you." She had gone with big, bigger, and biggest to describe her drink sizes for the 12, 16, and 20 ounce size cups. She enjoyed being different. It was what set her apart.

As she was making the drink, she noticed Clyde come in. Clyde was fairly rotund with thinning hair and a few teeth shy of a mouthful. He clearly was missing a few in the brains department as well. Some said he was just a little slow because he took drugs when he was younger while others said he was disabled. Willow wasn't sure which it was, but when he was around trouble usually followed close behind. And since her days as a murder suspect a few weeks before, Willow was trying to keep her nose clean. Which was, for some reason, really hard to do. Because trouble also liked to follow her around. Put her and Clyde in the same room together and trouble pretty much was a guarantee.

She watched him carefully.

He walked straight to Mr. Rune's table and started speaking and gesturing with his hands. The way he talked, in a kind of a slow whine, made it difficult for Willow to hear.

The blender mixing the frap didn't help her ability to hear either. She turned the blender off and filled the glass, topped it off with whipped cream and a drizzle of chocolate and caramel, stuck a straw in it, then took it to Mitch who was already setting up. She couldn't help it if Mr. Rune's table was near the stage, could she?

She had no idea Clyde knew Mr. Rune. None whatsoever. She was close enough to hear the words "money, cheated, never again," and "you'll pay." *Hmm…wonder what happened between the two of them?*

[8]

Clyde left right after speaking with the author. Mr. Rune went back to his writing like nothing had happened. Maybe this time she was wrong. Maybe Clyde hadn't brought trouble with him.

Mitch finished setting up and a few minutes later Mr. Rune ordered another coffee, although this time, it was to go. He knew it was about to get loud and, well, loud wasn't the writer's style. He gathered up his belongings and put them in his leather brief case, and took his coffee and left. She wouldn't see him until after the ice cream festival. She had tried to talk him into participating but he muttered something about deadlines, rewrites, and time, then shook his head and stalked off, obviously in a mood. She had thought perhaps having a famous writer's name attached to the ice cream festival would bring in some much needed income for the town.

The other writer in town, Jasper James, volunteered to help. Willow was glad for the help, but, because the writer wasn't well known, he wasn't going to attract a crowd like Huxley Rune would have. *Oh well, you can't have it all.*

6:30. 30 minutes until show time. She opened the glass partition and one of her part timers helped her rearrange the tables and chairs, making sure there was plenty of room for all who wanted to attend.

Willow was surprised to see Clyde return. He ordered a chocolate milk shake, found a table, and waited for the fun to begin.

Karaoke was in full swing. Willow had brought in two of her part timers and Janie, her best friend who normally worked the morning shift to help with the crowd. Business was booming. She finally felt like she was starting to become part of the town. Last month's fiasco with the chili cook-off almost sent her packing.

She smiled as three teenage girls took the stage. The music started up and all three of them were giggling. As the music they chose filled the room, Clyde flew up out of his chair in a rage. He took long strides and approached the stage. He was shaking his head and telling them he didn't like the song they were singing. This time Willow got involved.

"Clyde, leave the girls alone."

"This isn't an appropriate song. They have to stop singing this song."

Willow recognized the song as an upbeat song sung by the Dixie Chicks. Apparently some people still harbored bitterness over the chicks' political position they took years ago. "Clyde, the girls aren't making a political statement. They are just singing a fun song about a guy named Earl. Leave them alone."

He walked back to his table, complaining as he went. "They shouldn't sing this song. It's not right. This is a celebration in America. We shouldn't sing songs like that. It's a bad song."

Willow understood. Back in the day she hadn't been pleased about the route the singing group took in expressing their opinions either. In fact, she threw away the cds she owned of theirs. But, years had passed and she'd learned you have to forgive and move on or the bitterness would eat you up. Besides, the Earl song was fun. It even made her smile.

As soon as she was behind the counter, the loud pounding music came to an abrupt halt. The entire system had stopped working. She scanned the room and found Clyde on his hands and knees by the electrical outlet. She blew out an aggravated breath then confronted Clyde.

"Clyde, you are done here. You are not welcome in my shop. You are banned."

He started to protest. "That is a bad song. You shouldn't let them sing that song. Earl Rune had to die. It's a bad song."

Willow thought she heard him wrong. "Clyde, did you say the song is about Earl Rune? Mr. Rune's first name is Huxley, not Earl. Okay?

The song isn't about Mr. Rune. The song is just pretend. Someone made it up. It's not about anyone in particular." She paused to see if he was listening to her. "You need to go home, Clyde. We'll talk tomorrow to see if you are banned. I don't want to ban you but you can't be doing things like that. It isn't polite."

"Earl Rune had to die. Earl Rune had to die." He muttered again as he left the coffee shop.

Chapter 2

Willow watched through the window front as Embry's car slowly passed the shop. She chuckled. Parking spaces near the shop were at a premium. Even the private ones behind the building were already filled up. *Good luck, little girl.* Willow laughed when she saw her car pass again going the opposite direction. She'd probably have to park at the middle school and either walk or flag down one of the volunteers with access to a golf cart.

She went back to stocking her shelves. Today could very well be the busiest day of the year and a day that could give the shop a little nest egg for the future. She, along with her three part timers, Kenzie, Paige, and Gloria, her best friend, Janie, and her daughter, Embry, were all on staff today. The morning had already seen lines standing outside the door and down the sidewalk.

Embry walked through the door 15 minutes later. "Better late than never!" She called out to anyone listening as she disappeared through the office door to put her things away.

Upon returning, Willow handed Embry her apron. "Here you go. I made this one just for you."

"Mom, you took up sewing?"

"No, let me rephrase that. I had this made just for you."

Embry laughed. "That's what I thought." She unfolded the apron. "You remembered!" She read the little ditty out loud. "I scream, you scream, we all scream for ice cream." It had a big triple dip ice cream cone on the front.

"I had these made up to surprise you. Everyone got one a little different from the others. Yours, of course, just had to have your favorite childhood chant when you wanted a blue moon ice cream cone. You were quite annoying at times."

"I learned from the best." Embry smiled, kissed her mother's cheek, and jumped in to wait on customers.

The park across the street was beginning to fill up. The carnival rides were still, waiting for the start time. Although the event didn't officially start until early evening, people were walking around anticipating the fun they would have with their families. The whole downtown area was hopping. Willow Tree Ice Cream and Coffee Shoppe was on Main Street which ran directly through the middle of town. Her shop and the park were at one end of the street and Molly's Café was at the other end. Everything else; the library, police station, city hall, and the fire department, was in-between.

Willow had talked to Molly that morning and found out she had to send someone on an emergency run for more supplies. Business was booming for both of them. They both decided it was a good problem to have. Her marketing worked. It was about time she put her college degree to good use. Even without the help of Mr. Rune, her little town would see a record number of visitors thanks to her efforts.

Later in the afternoon there would be traditional contests like the three legged race and the potato sack race, among others and families would be spread out listening to the bands scheduled to play while picnicing. The dunk tank had been filled and was waiting for its first victim. She was even hosting a karaoke contest, despite the problems the night before with Clyde. She shook her head. *What in the world was he talking about? Earl Rune had to die? Nonsense.*

Willow wanted to check on command central. She was the official hostess for the Ice Cream Festival and it was her duty to make sure everything was operating smoothly. She called out to Janie, "I'm gonna walk over to the park for a little bit. You all good here?"

[15]

Janie waved her on. "Go. It's good to get out among the people. Besides, don't you have work to do for the festival? You aren't supposed to be locked up in here waiting on people." She looked around at her cohorts. "Isn't that what we're all here for?"

"Okay, okay, I'm going." She held up her phone. "If you need me, give me a call."

Willow walked outside and turned her face toward the sun. It was already warm enough to send sweat droplets skittering down her spine. In a couple of hours she would be covered in perspiration. She had to agree with one of her younger customer's exclamations. Every day he came in for an ice cream cone and every day he said, "I feel like a hotdog on a grill." She didn't bother asking him how he knew what a hotdog felt like. She understood the sentiment perfectly. Those 100 degree days were unheard of in the north. She wished she was independently wealthy and could afford a summer house in Door County, located in the thumb of the north east part of the state of Wisconsin. Beautiful country. Alas, that was not the case so she would have to acclimate.

Willow crossed the street, waving to people as she walked. Her place in the community had been sealed when she cleared her own good name and revealed Annabelle Butterfield as a murderer.

She'd just as soon forget the whole ordeal and serve up dishes of ice cream and creamy lattes. A much better way to spend her days than dealing with murder.

The craft show vendors were setting up. She stopped to admire some bookshelves. "These are beautiful!" She ran her hand over the intricately carved book case. "Do you make them?"

"I do." He handed her a business card. "I'm Vick. Nice to meet ya."

She glanced at the price tag and let out a low whistle. So much for getting one for the coffee shop. She had been thinking of putting in a shelf of books for her patrons, and one of the shelves in front of her would be beautiful in the shop, but she couldn't afford that price.

"I mostly do custom work. I normally don't do craft fairs."

"Good idea. It'll get your name out there, let people get to know your work. Do you live here in Turtle?"

"No, I live a couple of towns over. About 20 miles from here."

"Well, welcome to Turtle's ice cream festival. The crowds will be crazy tomorrow." She smiled at him then moved to the next vendor.

The petting zoo was getting their fence put together. Classic cars lined the street. The only negative about being the chairwoman for this year's event was she couldn't enter the homemade ice cream contest. Willow wasn't happy but she managed to talk Embry into entering. That would have to suffice for this year. Willow did not approve of her flavor, but, beggars couldn't be choosy. Bacon and Waffle Ice Cream. Who ever heard of such a thing?

She shrugged her shoulders and continued to walk around, checking to see if anyone needed anything as she went. Steve caught up with her as she walked. He was going to be the main attraction for the dunk tank. She wanted to be first in line. He had no idea but she was a pitcher for her softball team in high school. And she had been practicing.

"Buy me a coffee?"

She tilted her head. "What happened to the southern gentleman routine?"

He grinned. "If I remember correctly, you bribed me to do this water tank gig with free coffee for a month. I'm just getting what is coming to me."

"Oh yeah. I kinda forgot about that." She laughed. "Good thing you didn't."

"Like I'm going to forget something like free coffee? I don't think so."

She led him back to her shop and poured him a cup of regular joe. He took a drink. "Mmm, this tastes good."

Embry interrupted. "Mom, my ice cream is in the walk in. I'd like to check it. Do you mind unlocking it for me?" She had placed her homemade ice cream in the freezer for tomorrow's contest and needed to make sure it had set up correctly.

"Oh, sure. Steve, I'll be right back."

She grabbed her keys and led Embry to the walk-in the city rented for the event. The lock was dangling from the handle, open. "I could have sworn I locked this before I closed it up yesterday afternoon."

She pulled the door open and she and Embry each took turns looking from the contents of the freezer to one another, screaming in rotation. Mr. Rune was sitting on a bin of pistachio ice cream, his face was covered with frost. Even his eye lashes had crystals in them. His eyes were wide and looked like glass. His mouth fully open, as if Mr. Rune died at the very moment his scream came to life.

The first words to pop into Willow's head were, "Earl Rune had to die."

Chapter 3

Willow studied the scene in front of her as Embry ran for Steve, who happened to still be sipping his coffee in the shop. Mr. Rune's briefcase was lying open and various papers were strewn about the freezer floor. She was careful not to touch anything as she bent closer to get a better view. She heard Steve approach from behind her.

"You're just a magnet for murder, aren't you?"

"Me? I didn't do anything." She wrinkled her brow. "Besides, how do you know he was murdered? Maybe he was wanting a scoop of pistachio ice cream."

He ignored the first part of her comment and tossed her a wry look. "What else would it be? Do you think he went for a walk and accidently froze to death in the walk in freezer?"

She faked being offended. "Fine. It's murder. I don't see his manuscript. He had it when he left the coffee shop last night. And those are the same clothes he was wearing so I'm assuming he didn't get too far after leaving here."

Steve stepped closer to the frozen screaming corpse. "Mr. Rune, what were you doing in the walk in freezer?"

Willow added to his question. "And who put you in here then secured the door with an unlocked lock?"

"There was no lock?"

"Well, there was a lock. It was just loosely hanging on the fixture. Like someone was interrupted and unable to finish locking the door."

Steve stepped outside to view the door handle. "We'll need to try and get some prints from this door." He studied her for a moment. "Who besides you had access to the key?"

"I keep the key on my keyring. No one has asked me for them." She turned from clue searching to scrutinizing Steve's face. "Hey, come on. You don't think I killed him, do you?"

"Of course not. You don't have a motive, do you?"

She put her hands on her hips. "No, I don't."

"Well, good. Then you don't have anything to worry about, then do ya?"

Willow walked around outside the trailer looking for anything that might give any indication what Mr. Rune was doing in the parking lot behind her shop. It wasn't as if there was anything of interest back there. Just a place where she and her employees parked their cars, some overgrown weeds growing through the cracks of the asphalt, and the dumpster. She tapped herself on the forehead. "The dumpster."

She peered over the edge, looking for anything out of place. "Nothing. I see nothing but our normal trash."

She turned toward Steve then caught sight of something out of the corner of her eye. A cup. A cup sitting on the ledge of the window. "Steve, over here."

She heard him talking to another police officer and probably the coroner. Talk about putting a damper on today's ice cream festival.

"What did you find?" His voice interrupted her dwelling on the ramifications of a murder, today of all days.

"I found his coffee from last night. He always takes one to go." She pointed at the cup. "See, that's his initials and it still has most of the coffee in it. And it would appear he set it there on purpose, like he needed to have his hands free to do something else." She looked around. "But, what?"

She found Steve grinning at her. "You've become quite the little deductive detective, haven't you?"

"I wonder who he was helping." She turned in a circle. "He had to have been lured back here. He wouldn't have come back this way on his own. There wouldn't have been a reason to. And, it must have been someone he trusted. Huxley wasn't a person to go out of his way to help someone he didn't know. He was really introverted." She added. "And shy."

"You sound like you knew him pretty well."

"No, not really. I just observed him. Since I added the coffee line, he has been coming in almost every day to write. I just watched him interact with people. He never initiated contact. He was pleasant, but, standoffish. Aloof, yet approachable. If that makes sense."

"I can appreciate that. I've heard writers are a pretty secluded bunch." He bagged the cup. Coffee and all and handed it over to one of his officers. "We'll try and clear the crime scene as soon as we can." He started to walk away. "If you think of anyone, anyone at all in your observations of Mr. Rune that might be a suspect, let me know."

"Oh my goodness. I almost forgot." She told him about Clyde's interaction with Huxley then his weird behavior after returning to the coffee shop. "I had no idea what to make of what he said. I just wrote it off. Perhaps I shouldn't have."

Steve wrote down Willow's statement, as if interviewing a witness. Which, technically, she was. Just as he was finishing up, they both heard a commotion and turned toward the back door of the shop. Gloria was running toward the walk in freezer.

"No, it can't be Huxley. It can't be him." She was yelling as she ran. A police officer stopped her before she could contaminate the crime scene.

Willow looked at Steve. "I didn't even know she knew Mr. Rune."

Chapter 4

Willow took Gloria by the arm. "Come in and sit down. I had no idea you were that close to Mr. Rune." She poured her a cup of hot tea.

Gloria's eyes widened. "I'm not close to him. Why would you think that?"

"From your reaction. I can understand being upset, he was a customer of ours. You almost seemed like you were in shock like you'd lost your best friend or something. I would have guessed you knew him really well."

"No, I didn't." She sipped her tea. "I just love his books. I mean, I've read everything he has written and it's such a tragedy to lose someone so talented." Gloria looked up. "Have you read *Murder at Midnight*? It's the best book ever."

Willow shook her head. "You certainly didn't act like a star struck fan. I have never even seen you wait on him."

"Oh, I was too nervous to wait on him. I just worshipped from afar."

Gloria was fairly new to both her job and to the little town of Turtle. Willow didn't know her that well. "You moved here from out east, didn't you? Was it New Jersey?"

Gloria stared for just a moment before answering. "Yes, I did. I wanted a fresh start in life."

Willow wondered what she needed a fresh start from but didn't question her on that subject. "In your "worshipping from afar" did you ever notice anyone threatening Mr. Rune? Anyone who had anything against him? Anyone that wanted to hurt him?"

"Not that I noticed. But, I could look on Facebook for you and see if anyone threatened him there. Sometimes Facebook can get pretty heated."

Steve returned from outside and joined them.

Willow raised her eyebrows and spoke to Gloria. "Do you think you're okay enough to return to work? Or would you rather go home?"

She glanced between Steve and Willow. "I'd like to go home, if that is all right?"

Willow nodded. "Sure, go ahead. I'm sure we'll be okay." Although she highly doubted it as there was already a large group of people gathered trying to get inside. Most probably looking for gossip, but as Willow had previously experienced, some would buy something to justify their quest.

Thankfully, Embry worked hard enough for two people.

Willow watched as Gloria gathered her things and left through the back door. She thought back to the evening before. Huxley left right at 9 pm. It was just dark outside and karaoke was starting. She looked at her posted schedule. Gloria clocked out at 8:30. Surely she would have been gone by 9, right?

She looked up to see Steve studying her. "You have an idea?"

"No, more a concern. Something isn't sitting right with Gloria. Something about her story isn't adding up."

"You want to take a ride with me? I'm going to head over to the Rune residence."

"You'd let me do that?"

"My thinking is if I let you go with me it'll keep you from breaking and entering." He grinned showing that dimple, lighting up her own smile. "Am I right?"

"Yeah, great idea. Let me grab my purse." She turned to Janie. "I'll be back in a little while. I've got to run an errand."

Just as Steve parked across the street from Huxley's house, a hooded trespasser ran out the side door and through the back yard, climbed the fence and disappeared through the neighbor's back yard.

"Someone beat us here." He called in what little description he had then approached the door which was still open. He turned to Willow. "You stay here while I make sure it's clear." The look he gave her said he was serious.

She waited until he gave the all clear then started in on the room with the side door, the kitchen. The room was nice and neat. No trash in the can. No dirty dishes. Nothing out of place. He had cans of soup lined up like little toy soldiers in one cupboard. The refrigerator held some half and half, a block of cheddar cheese, and some yogurt. On the counter was a fruit basket with a few apples and a few oranges. She couldn't find a single sweet in the place. Not even a hidden stash of chocolate pushed back where no one could see it. *Who lives like this?*

Willow opened a bottom cupboard. "Oh my goodness. Look what I found."

Steve appeared in the doorway a few seconds later. "What did you find?"

Willow held out a green container with a domed lid for him to view.

"I don't get it. You'll have to explain."

"It's a lettuce keeper. My mom used to have one and our lettuce never went bad. Do you know how fast lettuce goes bad? Sometimes before I can use it. Seriously. These things are amazing."

Steve gave her a bewildered look. "Willow, what does this have to do with the case?"

"Oh. It doesn't. I just forgot all about this and when I saw it, I kind of got excited."

He shook his head. "Over lettuce." He turned and called out. "I'll be in the office looking for clues. Quit touching stuff. Your fingerprints will be all over this place. Or at least put on the gloves I gave you." He disappeared around the corner.

Willow moved on to the bedroom and tried to maintain focus. Rune's top dresser drawer was hanging open and the contents were a mess, like someone had been rummaging through the drawer. Probably the person they just interrupted. *What in the world were they doing in his underwear?*

She opened the nightstand drawer and pulled out a leather bound book. The first line read, "She followed me to this little town and this is probably where I breath my last."

"Steve, I found something."

He looked around the corner of the door way. "For real this time?"

She held up the diary. "You're going to want to read this." She held it out to him.

[29]

"Thankfully our intruder friend didn't find this before we did or we may have never seen it."

He read some of the first page. "Huh, sounds like he has a stalker. Wonder who she is?"

Willow shook her head. "I have no idea. If she follows him to the coffee shop I've never seen her."

Steve stood. "I found something too. Come on." He motioned for her to follow him.

"All right fearless leader. Lead on."

He knelt in front of the fire place. "Look at this." He had separated a few pieces of burned papers from the ashes. One of them was obviously the top of a title page. The title and author had white out underneath and Murder Beneath was the new title and Huxley Rune was the new author.

"Huh. So, first, why did someone destroy this and second, why did he white out his own name? I can understand the title, perhaps he changed his mind about that, but his name? That makes no sense." She looked at each of the remaining pieces and shook her head. "There are no answers here. Just more questions."

She put the pieces into the plastic bag Steve gave her then heard car doors.

Willow was about to leave when she noticed the woodwork lining the fireplace. She ran her hand along the same beautiful book shelves she'd seen at the craft fair. She was certain this was Vick's work. The style and quality were exactly the same. She'd have to ask him how he knew Mr. Rune.

"Come on. The team is here to finish up. We can get going." He met the police officers at the door. "You are not going to steal from a dead man, are you?"

Willow guiltily put the lettuce keeper back in the cupboard. "No, of course not. I was going to offer his heir a few dollars." She returned his scowl. "Oh come on. It's not worth more than a few bucks. Think rummage sale prices." She closed the cabinet door and stomped out of the house.

While driving home, Steve's phone rang. "Hello, Mrs. Frost. How are you today?" He waited a moment while she explained her problem. "Okay, I'll be right over. I do have someone with me, is that okay? All right then, we'll be there in a few minutes."

Steve looked to Willow. "Sorry about this, but we have to stop by the Frost residence. It seems Mrs. Frost has had a robbery."

"Oh, I hope it's not something serious. We seem to be having a crime wave in our little town. First Delonda, now Mr. Rune, and a burglary. What is next?

"I'm sure it's just a prank. Too many youngsters running around with nothing to do but cause trouble."

He pulled his truck in front of the little cottage style house and managed to open Willow's door before she could. She was learning.

Mrs. Frost met them on the front porch. "We have to go to the back yard." She hobbled down her front steps.

Willow suppressed a chuckle as the short stout woman waddled to her back yard in her slippers and housecoat. Her hair was in pink spongy curlers with a bright pink bandana covering most of the curlers and tied under her chin. She was quite the sight.

"See? They're all gone."

Willow was lost. "What is gone?"

"My laundry, that's what. It's all gone. I hung it on the line yesterday early evenin' then I got one of my famous headaches, hurt like the dickens too, and I laid down to rest. Well, I plumb forgot about my unmentionables hanging out on the line. And my best housecoat too. Until this afternoon when I went outside and saw all the clothespins on the ground. Look at em' all. Do you know how long it took me to hang up all those unmentionables? Do you see how crooked my fingers are from that doggone arthritis?"

She pointed to the wooden fasteners lying on the ground, pretty much directly under the taught rope. "Who would do such a thing? What would they want with my bloomers? Now I'm gonna have to go to the city to buy some more."

Willow tried to imagine the person who would steal this woman's underwear. Her mind searched the known world and came up with no one. Not a soul.

Steve seemed to be speechless. Willow elbowed him.

He took out his notepad. "Um, can you describe the items stolen?"

Willow busted out laughing. Mrs. Frost gave her a look that immediately shut her up and caused her eyes to widen.

"Well, I have pink ones. They're so soft and satiny. I have green and blue ones too. I also hung out my good cotton ones with little pink and blue flowers. There were three of them. Almost all my bloomers were dirty. You get to be my age and, well, accidents happen. You'll see. My housecoat. It's yellow with blue birds on it. My sister sent it to me from Idaho for Christmas last year. It has two pockets on the front. I love it cause I can put my hankie and my new cell phone in there. It's just the bee's knees. Somebody got themselves the jackpot."

Steve promised he would be on the lookout for her underwear. How in the world he would do that, Willow had no idea. Perhaps he would have random underwear checks. The thought caused a fit of giggles.

"You can stop now. You really can."

She held her stomach. "No, I can't." Then laughed harder.

With the surprise element of undergarments being stolen, Steve forgot to ask her if she knew where Clyde was. As much as he hated to, after dropping Willow at the shop he headed back to talk to Clyde's mother, Mrs. Frost.

Chapter 5

Willow jumped behind the counter and started waiting on customers. The line was out the door and half way down the block. *Boy, news sure does travel fast.*

"Hi, Martha. I didn't think I'd see you out tonight. How are you?" Willow wanted to reach out with a pair of scissors and cut her hair. One side was always a little longer than the other and it drove Willow crazy.

"Oh, I'm fair to middlin'."

"That good, huh?" Willow chuckled. Martha had to be the quietest person she knew. She leaned in closer to hear what else she had to say. "By the way, who cuts your hair?" Willow couldn't resist.

Martha Claremont put her hand to her chin length hair and touched it. "I go to the Red Robin in the city. I've been going for years."

Willow made a mental note to remember that name.

Martha leaned forward and whispered, "Is it true? Is Mr. Rune dead?"

She sobered. "Yes, it's true. We found him in the walk-in freezer."

"Was he three sheets to the wind?"

Willow hadn't thought of that. Perhaps the man had a tolerance for alcohol that gave the impression he was sober when in fact, he was unable to function with all his faculties in order. She had heard of people who put on a real good show when they were drunk out of their mind. "I don't know. I suppose that could be the case. I hadn't really considered it. I think Chief Grice will make sure they run a full toxicology report on him."

Willow changed the subject. "How is your book club going?"

Martha mumbled something unintelligible then turned to leave.

Willow called out after her. "Martha, did you want your tea?" She held the cup out to her.

Martha took the cup without a word then walked out the front door.

"Huh, wonder what her problem is?"

Janie spoke over her shoulder. "I think she tried to get Huxley to participate in one of their club meetings and he refused. At least that's the rumor going around. She wasn't too happy about it."

"I bet not."

Willow waited until the line of nosy patrons had been taken care of and ventured away. She wanted to talk to Vick once more, to see if he admitted to making the shelving unit around Mr. Rune's fireplace. If not, she wondered what he had to hide.

The crowd was gathering, even with the untimely passing of their resident writer. It wasn't as if anyone from town really knew him. He was a loner and he was new to the area. He hadn't made any real friends that she knew of. No wonder people didn't seem to be affected by his death. Besides Gloria, that is. And Martha. She seemed stunned by the news.

"Hi there. I see you're back. Change your mind about the shelves?"

Willow waved. "Maybe. I'll have to save for a bit, but it might be workable. I would love to have some made for the coffee shop." She didn't have to pretend to be interested. They were absolutely beautiful and she really would love to have them for her shop. "Did you hear the bad news?"

"Oh, yeah. About that writer dying? I overheard a lady talking about it."

"Did you know him? The writer, that is?"

He shook his head. "No, I don't think so. What was his name?"

"Huxley Rune." She watched him carefully for any sign he was lying but saw nothing. Either the guy really didn't know Huxley or he was an excellent liar. She couldn't tell which.

"No, I can't say that I've heard of him. Do you know what he's written?"

Willow shook head. "He writes mysteries. I know that much."

Deciding not to push her luck, Willow wished him well and continued walking. The carnival rides were piping music throughout the park and people were wandering around eating cotton candy, caramel apples, and funnel cakes. Others were eating barbecue on picnic tables. Every now and again she noticed a couple with a blanket and a picnic basket. Everyone was eating. Except her.

"Hey. Want a bite?" She turned around to see Steve holding out chicken on a stick for her to sample.

"Are you eating again?" She took a bite of the moist chicken.

"What do you mean, again? My coffee got interrupted and I never received my cinnamon roll. This is my breakfast and lunch. He stretched his neck trying to get a better view of the pile of nachos passing him by. "Oh, that looks good."

She agreed with him although she didn't let him know that. "We have a murder to solve. And tomorrow, if my walk in freezer is still a crime scene, I'm going to need a new one and a lot more ice cream. I've got other things to think of besides my stomach.

A large walking ice cream sundae stopped in front of them and waved. Both Steve and Willow waved back and walked around it.

"Hey, my stomach doesn't talk, it shouts. And I've got no choice but to listen. Besides, who says I'm not working? A man has to eat." He took another bite. "I stopped by Clyde's. His mom hasn't seen him all day. My men are watching for him. Do you think he took off?"

She considered his question. "No. Where would he go?"

The ice cream sundae was following them. Willow looked over her shoulder and waved once more. "Have you noticed the creepy ice cream dude following us?" She whispered.

I'm trying to ignore it. Thanks." He upped his pace. "I came to the same conclusion. He has nowhere else to go. He's probably at the carnival.

She took the stick from him and kept walking while she ate. "He doesn't have anyone besides his mom. And he's not capable of making it on his own. She stopped walking and turned in a slow circle, looking for Clyde. The ice cream person was still watching her.

Steve looked from his empty hand to Willow's chewing mouth and started leading her toward the food trucks. "What if he wasn't trying to kill him? What if he was trying to shut him up? Or put him in a time out? I heard his mom still uses that method of discipline with him. Could be he was doing the same thing."

"I don't know. You should have heard him at the shop yesterday evening. He was mad. Then he took it out on those poor high school girls. They were so embarrassed. Sort of took the fun out of the whole evening." She stopped walking and pointed at the walking ice cream sundae. "I think he's fully capable of murder. I don't think people give him enough credit and I think he's smarter than he lets on. She started pursuing the waddling suited dish. "And who do you think might be in that ice cream suit?"

"No, it can't be. I've walked by that guy at least a dozen times. He's been following us around like a lost puppy."

"Let's find out, shall we?"

Willow fell into step behind the scurrying ice cream. The cherry topping from the costume covered the costume wearer's head and since the fleeing sundae was avoiding confrontation, Willow reached up and pulled the top off.

"Willow, what'd you do that for?" Clyde whined.

"Clyde, I've been looking everywhere for you."

"That's dumb. I've been here the whole time."

"Police Chief Grice has been trying to find you. He wants to ask you a few questions about Mr. Rune."

Clyde took the top of his costume from Willow. "You're gonna get me in trouble. I'm supposed to be walking around and having my picture taken with the little kids."

"This is important, Clyde. And it will only take a few minutes. I promise."

"Oh, all right, fine. What do you want?"

Steve cleared his throat. "Clyde, I need to ask you about the other night in the coffee shop, when you got into an argument with Mr. Rune."

"Okay."

"What were you arguing about?"

"He didn't pay me. That's not nice. If you want someone to do work for you, then you have to pay. That's how it works. My mama told me that."

"Yes, that is correct. You said something that night to Willow. You said Earl Rune had to die. Do you remember saying that?"

Clyde became visibly agitated. "I have to go back to work now. I can't talk about that. I can't talk about that. I have to go to work."

Chief Grice tried to calm him down. "Clyde. It's okay. Let's sit down, okay? Do you want a soda?" Clyde grinned. "I'm awfully hot in this ice cream suit. Can I have a soda?"

Steve nodded and caught one of the mobile vendors with a tray of soft drinks. "Here you go. Take a drink and that will help you cool down." He waited for Clyde to drink half the cup before proceeding. "Now, can you tell me about last night? What did you see?"

"I didn't see Mr. Rune get hurt. I didn't see him fall to the ground. I promise."

Willow handed him another soda. "Clyde, who hurt Mr. Rune? Who made him fall to the ground?"

"My mama didn't do it. She didn't do it. She didn't hurt Mr. Rune." Clyde ran for the carnival forgetting that his legs were confined by the odd shape of the costume he was wearing. He tumbled, rolled, and then came to a stop face down. A couple of bystanders helped him to his feet and he waddled as fast as he was able , leaving both Willow and Police Chief Grice speechless.

Chapter 6

Willow woke to Clover barking her head off.

"I'm up. I'm up." She plodded to the door and let the dog outside then she turned the coffee pot on. No climbing back into bed today. Not with the ice cream festival in full swing.

Clover liked to roam outside while Willow readied herself. It had become something of a ritual. She poured herself a cup of the strong brew and took it to the bathroom with her. Twenty minutes later, she was dressed and ready for another blistering day.

"Clover." She yelled out the back door. "Come on." She had converted part of her utility room into a dog zone. Clover loved the freedom and she hadn't gotten into too much trouble. At least not yet.

Willow closed the door then started for her truck. Halfway there, she stepped in a hole the size of Texas. "Clover!" *Ugh. That dog has been digging holes again.* She stretched and rotated her ankle, hoping she didn't sprain it. She had too much to do to be down. *That darn dog.*

She hobbled the remaining distance to her truck and promised herself she would figure out how to keep Clover from digging. First, she had a festival to get underway. The new freezer rental was supposed to be delivered by the time she got to the shop. The ice cream factory was sending over all new drums of ice cream as well. The old one was a crime scene. What the police thought they were going to do with all that ice cream she didn't know, but it was their problem now. As long as Steve didn't try to pawn it off on her after they were finished with it, she was all good.

The new freezer was a thing of beauty. Willow sighed a breath of relief as she pulled in behind her shop and saw the new one all set up. She glanced at her watch. She had an hour before the ice cream would be delivered. The back door was already open. Of course Janie beat her to work. She probably had all the cinnamon rolls made too. Willow could smell the sweet bread from her car door.

She put her purse in the office and let out a grunt. Sitting on her desk was a small pint of pistachio ice cream, make that melted ice cream that had found its way to her desk calendar, and the invoices she had left sitting out.

Willow followed her nose to the kitchen. "Hey, did you put a container of ice cream on my desk?"

"Well, good morning to you too. And no, I didn't."

"Huh, that's weird. I wonder who did. It isn't even the brand we use."

"What flavor is it?"

"Pistachio." Willow put her hand to her mouth.

Janie nodded. "Wasn't that the flavor Mr. Rune was sitting on in the freezer?"

"It sure was. You don't think…"

"I do. Someone is trying to send you a message. And I don't think it's a love letter either."

She shook her head then called Steve. He didn't answer.

A few minutes later Steve arrived. He sat at down at a table as Janie approached with the coffee pot.

"Your usual?"

"No, I think I'm going to have one of those cinnamon bran muffins Willow was telling me about. Perhaps I should start eating healthier."

"Ya know, I didn't think I'd like them, but they're really good. Of course, I do smother them with butter. Want it warmed up?"

He grinned. "Baby steps."

She laughed and went for his muffin.

Willow sat down beside him. "Janie getting your cinnamon roll?"

"Nope. Not having one today."

She gave him an odd look. A few weeks ago she thought there might be something developing between them, something more than friendship. Now, while his dimple still caused her to catch her breath, he was more like a good friend, or an older brother. Not that she would be hard to convince otherwise. She was simply taking her cues from him.

"Then what are you having?"

"I'm trying that new muffin you told me about. The bran one."

"Good for you." She went and poured herself a cup of coffee then returned. "What have you found out about Huxley Rune? Any exes out for revenge? Anyone in his past that would rise up to bite him?"

Steve raised his eyebrows. "Well, apparently he moved because of that stalker situation out east, or at least that is what his agent said. He has never been married and he has no children. He had filed several complaints on a woman named Mary Jo Johnson. When he moved away she seemed to vanish into thin air. According to his journal, she followed him here. The only thing is, I haven't heard of a Mary Jo living in the area. Have you?"

"Nope, not a word."

Willow grew silent as Gloria dropped off their muffins. "Janie said to make sure you got these." She set the small plates down along with a small cup of butter then refilled their coffee cups. Afterward, she unlocked the front door for the coffee seekers standing outside.

"Looks like you've got quite the crowd. Murder hasn't been too bad for business this time around."

She scowled then moved behind the counter to help out. "Why don't you make yourself useful and go check out the gift someone left for me on my desk."

It was his turn to scowl. "What gift?"

"Come on, I'll show you."

After leaving Steve to examine the soggy ice cream container, Willow started helping Gloria make specialty coffees. "Hey, Gloria, did you already make the mocha?" Willow watched the woman next to her work. "Gloria? Hello? Gloria?" Finally she looked up.

"Oh, goodness. I'm so sorry. I was in my own little world. I didn't hear you."

Willow held up the ticket. "Did you already make the mocha? I can give you a hand."

Willow was surprised Gloria showed up for work. Especially after how she reacted to Mr. Rune's death the day before. She was thankful though. Business was going to be crazy busy. She needed every hand she could get. Embry was already taking orders and putting them out as fast as the rest of them could make the coffee. Their skills were going to be sorely tested.

Once the crowd was under control, Willow joined Steve who had already bagged the liquid ice cream and the container it came in.

"Are you sure one of your employees didn't put it there by accident? I would hate to waste tax payer's money."

"I'm sure. Janie was the only one here before me and I was the last one to leave last night. She didn't do it and I sure didn't do it. Nor is it the brand we sell." She pointed to the evidence bag in Steve's hand. "This can't be coincidence. Someone is trying to warn me away. I just know it."

"You've been watching too much Murder She Wrote. I take it you subscribe to Netflix?"

"What does that have to do with anything? And for the record, I happen to love Murder She Wrote."

She crossed her arms. The immediate crowd had been taken care of and everyone was scurrying around the kitchen getting ready for the next wave of customers. After lunch, Embry would need to leave and take her newly made ice cream to be judged. She wasn't too happy about having to do another batch since her first batch got confiscated with the crime scene.

Willow watched as Steve left with the melted ice cream then motioned for Embry to follow her. She caught Janie's eye and let her know they were stepping out. She had an idea and didn't want to alert too many people, especially Gloria. Steve would never approve of her tactics so she was glad he had a job to do. What he didn't know, wouldn't hurt him. And if she found anything, getting his forgiveness would be easier than getting his permission. At least she hoped he would see it that way.

She climbed behind the wheel of her truck and waited on Embry.

"Mom, where are we going?" She glanced at the time on her phone. "The ice cream contest starts in a couple of hours. I don't want to be late or I can't enter."

"Oh, you'll be back in plenty of time. Quit being a worry wart."

Embry rolled her eyes. "Can you at least tell me where we're going?"

"We're on a mission. I have a feeling someone isn't who they say they are."

Willow dialed her phone and left a voice mail. "Steve, can you do me a favor. Would you ask the police station back in New Jersey to fax you a picture of the woman who was stalking Huxley? Thanks."

"Mom, you don't have him on speed dial yet?"

"Hush. We have work to do."

She parked her truck a few houses down from the rental she knew to be Gloria's. "Come on. Let's go see exactly who Gloria is, shall we?" Willow led the way around the back of the house then tested the back door knob. "Darn. I was hoping it would be unlocked."

"You're breaking into someone's house? Seriously? What is your boyfriend going to think when he has to put you in jail?"

Willow made some inscrutable sound and used her elbow to break the glass.

Embry's mouth dropped. "I can't believe you just did that. I've only seen that done in the movies." She followed Willow into the house. "I'm going to go to jail too. I'm an accomplice."

"Would you stop whining and look around. Hurry up. Most of the town is at the festival but someone could have seen us and called the cops. I want to be out of here before they get here. Especially if it's Steve."

Willow took hold of Embry's hand and made her walk down the hall. "You take the door on the left, I'll get the one on the right. Look for anything obvious first, then, if need be we'll start rummaging through drawers."

Willow seemed to be in the master. Or at least the bedroom Gloria slept in. She heard her daughter call for her.

"Mom, you're gonna want to see this."

Willow crossed the hall and let out a whistle. The entire southern wall was covered in pictures of Huxley Rune. Coming. Going. Eating. Drinking. Shopping. There were even pictures of him in the shop. She never once saw Gloria go near him. Not once. Come to think of it, she had always made herself scarce when he was around. Her phone vibrated.

"Yeah? Oh, Hi Steve. Yes, I know. You're gonna want to see this." She paused for a second. "I'm at Gloria's. Mmhmm. I'll still be here." She pocketed her phone. "He's on his way."

"Can I go? I'll walk back."

Willow sighed. "Fine. Go."

Embry didn't have to be told twice. She took off through the back door and didn't look back. Willow was standing in front of the stalker wall of shame when Steve arrived.

"What in the world do you think you're doing?"

"Listening to my gut."

"Your gut is going to get you into trouble, you know that, right?"

He handed her the picture of Mary Jo. Willow compared the picture to the woman working in her shop. She had dyed her hair and was definitely wearing more make up, but there was no question. Gloria was Mary Jo.

"Good thing I got a warrant after taking a look at this picture. And I'm glad you didn't drag me along with you." He looked around. "Where did Embry go?"

"She thought you were going to put her in jail."

He smirked. "I should put you in jail."

"Oh come on. You should be thanking me. Without me you wouldn't even know who Mary Jo is."

"Give me a little credit, huh? I did manage to solve a few crimes before you became the resident professional sleuth."

She smirked. "Steve, look at this." She was still scrutinizing the wall of shame. "Looks like Ms. Mary Jo was our intruder at Mr. Rune's house. She has tacked burnt manuscript pages on her wall." She swallowed hard and pointed to the briefs hanging by a push pin. "I guess we now know why she was going through his underwear drawer. Thank goodness she didn't find his journal."

A police officer was taking pictures of the wall so Willow stepped backward, producing a pronounced creak in the floorboards. She raised her eyebrows then dropped to her knees. Sure enough, the floorboard was loose.

Steve motioned for another police officer, with gloves on, to check it out.

The officer pulled a clear plastic storage bag from the floor. Inside was Mary Jo's driver's license, her social security card, her passport, and her birth certificate.

"Wow. She really went to long lengths to convince us she is Gloria, didn't she? I have to say, she looks better in her current state as a brunette. She should keep it that way. Blond aged her too much." Willow was looking through some pictures, comparing them to Mary Jo's "Gloria" persona.

Steve started for the door, leaving the remaining officers to collect the evidence. "I have to get back to the station to question our suspect. I'll talk with you later."

"Don't you have to pick her up first?"

"See, there are some things you don't know. She's been sitting at the station for the past half hour."

"What? That means Janie and the two part timers are there by themselves. Sheesh. I gotta go." She started for her truck then called over her shoulder. "Call me if you need anything."

Willow noticed Embry's car was missing then guessed correctly she was at the ice cream contest. She hurried through the door.

Janie called out to her. "We're fine. A package was delivered for you. It's on your desk."

Willow ducked into her office and located a brown paper wrapped box. It was tied with twine and there was no sender address. Come to think of it, there was no delivery address. Not even a sticky note.

She cut the twine and unwrapped the package. Inside was a note.

"Willow, if you are reading this, then something has happened to me. Please safeguard this for me. My agent will be in touch. Regards, Huxley Rune."

Chapter 7

Willow couldn't believe she was holding the next best seller by Huxley Rune. And why in the world would he send it to her? Wasn't there someone else he trusted more than her? She barely knew him. And he barely knew her. It made no sense. She looked at the title and her eyes widened. It was the very same title the police chief rescued from the fireplace at Rune's place, Murder Beneath.

"What is going on?" She asked aloud.

She dare not leave the manuscript lying around. Who knows if it was the reason he was murdered. She put the copy in her safe and made sure it was locked before joining Janie and the others in the front. Business was still steady. Not quite out the door, like the morning rush, but all the tables were filled and there were people in line. She couldn't have asked for more.

Willow wanted to call Steve and let him know about the manuscript, but she dare not take the chance of anyone over-hearing her. She had to wait until she saw him in person, and alone.

The front door jingled and Gloria or Mary Jo, or whatever she was calling herself these days, walked in.

"Uh, Gloria. I didn't expect to see you so soon."

"Oh, yeah, that was nothing. Just a misunderstanding. I'm scheduled, right?"

Willow wasn't sure why Gloria was acting so indifferent. Did she really just call being taken in for questioning on a murder charge, nothing? Weird. "Why don't we go to my office and talk?"

Willow shut her office door then turned and faced Gloria. She remained silent, hoping Gloria would offer some sort of explanation without being prompted.

At first Gloria pretended to be clueless. Finally, she relaxed her shoulders and sighed. "I didn't kill him. I didn't. Why would I do that? I loved him. I moved a thousand miles to be near the man."

"Unrequited love has been known to drive people to desperate lengths. Perhaps you could no longer take the rejection?"

Gloria blew her bangs out of her eyes. "Never. I wouldn't hurt him. Not in a million years."

Willow thought about Gloria's reaction to his death. She truly was horrified and in shock.

That wasn't an act. Then again, what if she had a split personality and had no idea her evil twin killed him? *I've been watching too many crime shows. The real question is, what do I do about Gloria?*

"Have you been charged with any crime?"

"No, Police Chief Grice said to make sure I don't leave the area and I may be charged with breaking and entering. Maybe. But that is all he has on me. Everything else is circumstantial."

Willow sighed. "All right then, let's get back to work. I'm sure Janie could use the help." She didn't know what else to do. Her gut was telling her Gloria didn't kill him. But, it was also telling her Gloria wasn't altogether innocent either. What else could she do? She couldn't fire the woman simply because she might have killed Mr. Rune. Stalking on the other hand, well, she needed to talk with Steve. He would provide some much needed insight.

Embry came through the front door with a shout as Willow and Gloria took their places behind the front counter. "Mom, I took third."

Willow grinned. Like mother like daughter. Willow hugged her daughter. "Great job!"

Embry showed her the certificate. "I think I'll frame it, like yours." She laughed. "Maybe I'll enter next month's barbecue contest. You'll have some stiff competition."

"Bring it on, little girl." Willow turned. "Did you go by and let Clover out after the competition?"

"Of course. She was anxious to get out and dribbled on the floor. I cleaned up after her while she was running around outside." Embry paused a second. "Mom, you've got to do something about her digging holes. Someone is really going to get hurt."

Willow rotated her foot a little bit. It was a tender reminder of her own mishap with a Clover hole. Another thing she would have to talk to Steve about. So much to learn. So many things to do. Right now her priority was getting through the rest of the festival. "Yeah, this morning I managed to step in one myself. Twisted my ankle. Would have been horrible to have hurt it today of all days. I walked it off."

Willow turned when the bell on the door rang.

Jasper James was as exuberant as Huxley Rune was private. He entered Willow Tree Ice Cream Shoppe with a huge grin in place. "Bet you're glad you asked me to volunteer instead of old Rune." He pushed his cowboy hat down a little over his eyes and tried his best to be irresistible, which he did very well. Mr. James wrote westerns and he had a very high opinion of himself, both his writing and his good looks. And he wasn't too far off, at least in the looks department. Too bad he knew it. Willow had never read anything by him so she wasn't sure on that account.

"Hi, Mr. James. What can I help you with?"

He sauntered over to the counter where Willow was waiting. "Oh, I don't drink those fancy coffees. I'll have me a cola then I'll mosey on over to the round pen for the ropin' contest." He hooked his thumbs in his belt loops and widened his stance, his broken-in cowboy boots jingled as he moved. "I got me a whole passel of kiddos wantin' to rope them up a lil' dogie."

"We don't carry regular coke. But, we do have root beer which we use in our homemade ice cream floats. Would you like a frosty mug of that instead?"

"No, I'm not hankerin' for a root beer. How about I have a pistachio milkshake then." He leaned his back against the counter and looked around the room at his adoring fans. His moment of being the center of attention had passed and everyone was back in their own little world. He turned back to Willow with the corners of his mouth turned slightly downward.

She handed him his milkshake and watched him guzzle it down in one long breath. Was it public knowledge that Mr. Rune was found sitting on pistachio ice cream? She didn't think so.

"That was mighty fine. I thank ye." He turned and sauntered out the way he came in. Janie stood next to her. "Now there's a view."

Chapter 8

The next morning Willow tried to sleep in, only to be woken by a wet tongue in her ear. "Ew. Clover. Really? Do you know what time it is?"

She blinked hard to clear the sleep from her eyes and picked up the alarm clock to bring it closer. *Might be time to get reading glasses.* "It's 8:30, Clover. That's not sleeping in." She rolled over and screamed in her pillow. "Fine. But after you go, I'm going back to bed!"

Willow grudgingly let Clover out and ran for the bathroom. Getting older had its issues. Just the idea of going made her want to go, even if she didn't really have to. "Wonder if I could have one of those doggie doors installed." She muttered to herself as she watched her dog run around outside for her morning constitutional. She let the dog in then climbed back into bed. She needed more sleep. Willow's eyes popped open when her phone started buzzing. She had purposefully put it on vibrate hoping the annoying sounds emanating from the little device would be silenced while she caught up on some much needed sleep. She should have stuck it between some towels in the linen closet. The darn thing! The caller left a voice mail. She'd check later.

Willow snuggled deep into her pillow just as the phone vibrated again. Ugh!

"What?" She asked without looking at who was calling.

It was Janie. "You better get down here."

"Can't it wait? Sheesh. I'll be there in a few hours."

"This won't wait. Trust me."

Willow muttered as she pulled a pair of jeans on. "Seeing my second dead body in three weeks makes a girl tired. All I want is sleep." She checked Clover's water and food dish, ran a toothbrush over her teeth, a hairbrush through her hair then grabbed her keys and ran for the truck. Half way there, she fell in a hole. "Gosh darn it, Clover. This has got to stop!"

Willow's jaw dropped as she pulled into the parking lot of the ice cream shop. *The festival is over, where did all these people come from?*

She hustled in the back door and called out to Janie. "What in the world is going on?"

Janie answered, not caring if anyone in the seating area heard her. "One news team and a whole lot of groupies. Apparently our writer in demise had quite the following. Word got out.

Willow Tree Ice Cream Shoppe could become world famous. The murder is trending on Twitter."

Willow knew of Twitter, but didn't really understand it. "What does that mean?"

Janie explained it. "Hashtag is the pound sign symbol. It's used in front of a phrase that is being commonly talked about in the world. Things like, #Rune in ruins, #Mystery writer dead, and on and on it goes. It means people all over the world are talking about Huxley Rune being the subject of one of his own books. And your ice cream shop is smack dab in the middle of all the talk." She gestured around her. "Which is why the shop is packed and you need to put on an apron and help."

Willow quickly put an apron on and started taking orders. By the time 8 pm came, she was dead on her feet. One part timer was scheduled so the three of them worked straight through with no breaks. She hobbled on sore feet to her truck. Steve was leaning against the hood.

"I couldn't even get in the door. What was going on?"

She explained then shrugged her shoulders.

Steve smiled. He valued this woman's friendship. She was clearly exhausted. Probably hungry too. "You want to get something to eat?"

"I'm not sure which is winning, exhaustion or hunger."

"It'll do you good to sit down and relax. Wanna get something light at Molly's?" Sensing her propensity to decline, he threw in "And I can give you an update on the coroner's report."

Molly greeted them at the door. "Well, ain't you two a sight for sore eyes?" She held the door open. "Come on in. Honey, I heard you had quite the spectacle of onlookers." She led them to an open table. "Did you ever get the chance to sit a spell? I bet you could eat the north end of a southbound polecat. Let me get you fixed up." And off she went without asking either one of them what they wanted.

"I don't think I'm ever gonna understand that woman." Willow cocked her head in thought. "Did she just say I was hungry enough to eat a polecat's bottom?"

"Oh, give it time. You'll catch on. And yes, that is what she referenced." He laughed then picked up the menu even though he doubted he would need it.

A few minutes later, one of the waitresses brought out two large glasses of ice tea, two steaming bowls of corn chowder topped with bacon and grated cheddar cheese, and a basket of bread.

Willow lifted her spoon and lightly blew on the hot concoction. "She sure can cook."

Steve buttered the warm bread. "I'll second that."

"I'm glad she is the one running the cook-offs or I wouldn't stand a chance."

"Don't sell yourself short. I've tasted some mighty fine offerings from your neck of the woods." He ate a chunk of bread dipped in the soup.

"Okay, I'm all ears. Tell me what you have."

"Well, for starters, Mr. Rune froze to death. He was hit over the head and must have been placed in the walk in while unconscious. He probably woke up and sat down on the bucket of ice cream and froze in place. It's a wonder no one heard him. The interesting part is, he died just like one of the victims in one of his books. Not at an ice cream festival, mind you, but in a walk in freezer for a restaurant. The murderer has to be fan. It's not looking good for Gloria."

Willow nodded. "And as thin and wiry as he was, it wouldn't have taken a muscle man to drag him to the freezer. He couldn't have weighed 125 pounds soaking wet. Which means any one of our suspects could have done it. Even the ones who pretended they had no idea they knew him, which means Vick." She took the last bite of soup and rubbed her stomach. "That was delicious."

Their waitress removed the soup bowls just as Molly appeared with their meals.

"Molly, the soup was plenty."

Steve grimaced. "Speak for yourself." He took the plate of hot roast beef and held it close to his nose. "Oh, Molly. You're gonna have to wheel me out of here."

Willow bit into her roast beef and sighed. "I guess I was hungrier than I thought." She polished off the plate of tender beef and creamy mashed potatoes as though she hadn't eaten in a month of Sundays. Her eye lids were beginning to feel like the loaves of banana bread her part timer tried to make. Lead. Pure lead.

"Steve, I gotta get home before I drop right here."

"I'll drive you. We'll leave your truck at the shop and I'll pick you up in the morning. As tired as you are, you shouldn't be driving anyway."

She nodded. Not because she wanted to be dependent upon him for a ride, but because she couldn't argue. He was right. She just might fall asleep at the wheel and that wouldn't be good for anyone.

The next morning, Steve dropped Willow off at the front door of her shop then proceeded to the police station. As he walked in the station, the phone was ringing.

"Chief, it's Willow on the phone. You better get on back to the shop. Looks like someone gave her truck a new paint job."

Steve found Willow staring at the words written across the windshield of her truck. *You have something of mine* was brushed on the glass with pistachio green paint.

Chapter 9

"You have something of mine. I wonder what that means."

"I'm guessing Rune's latest manuscript."

Steve turned to look at her. "You have Huxley Rune's latest manuscript? When were you going to share this little bit of knowledge or did you think it wasn't important?"

Willow closed her eyes. "I forgot. I'm sorry. It was so hectic and I put it in my safe and just completely forgot about it. I swear. I didn't do it on purpose."

Steve took Willow by the shoulders. "Look at me. It's looking more and more like Huxley Rune was killed because of this manuscript. Merely having it puts you in imminent danger. As well as your employees. And your daughter." He figured that last statement would get her attention.

Embry, her morning help, chose that moment to pull into the parking lot.

Willow took one look at her daughter and started crying. Blubbering was more like it. All over the man. He was one snotty mess by the time she captured her emotions.

"Mom, what happened? What's wrong?" She looked at the message scrawled on her mom's windshield. "Who did this?"

"I don't know." She started crying all over again.

Willow started for the back door. "Come on. I'll put the coffee on." When she reached the door, she noticed it was already ajar. She stood completely still. "Steve. Steve." Her whisper was nearly silent. She had worked herself up into a fearful frenzy. Not the normal Willow she was used to being. Someone killed Huxley Rune and now they were after her.

Steve and Embry caught up to her. "What…" He stopped when he saw the door and motioned both women back to her truck then pulled his gun and slowly opened the door and disappeared inside. After a few minutes he stuck his head out the door. "Whoever it was is long gone. Come on inside. Tell me what is missing. But, don't touch anything."

Willow was appalled at the mess in her office. "I sure am working up a good mad." She looked around her office. Paperwork was strewn about. While her office had been trashed, she didn't notice anything missing. Until she looked in the corner under the high back chair. "My safe is gone."

"Are you sure?" Steve watched her face.

"Yep. I'm sure. I keep it under that chair and it's gone."

He bent down and sure enough, the safe was gone. "Okay, well, I'll need a list of what was in it."

She nodded and began to mentally recall what was stored for safe keeping. "The manuscript, of course. Embry's birthday list."

"Mom! Why would that be in your safe?"

"Because you are nosy and it's the only place I can keep a secret from you." She continued. "$500 in change for the shop, and a pearl necklace my mother left me. That's about it."

Steve finished his note. "Okay, if you think of something else, let me know." A couple of officers arrived on the scene and dusted for fingerprints and looked for anything that might lead them to the person who was wreaking havoc on their town.

Willow poured the three of them a cup of coffee then sat down at a small wrought iron table. "Oh my gosh. My safe wasn't stolen. I completely forgot I took it home." She bumped the table as she stood up and sent coffee sloshing all over the floor. "It's at home. I have to get home."

Steve caught up to her as she ran for her truck. "You can't take yours. They're still processing it. Come on, hop in mine." He used his siren to make record time to her house. As they pulled in with the sirens blaring, they saw a figure dressed in dark colors run for cover in the woods surrounding Willow's back yard.

Willow bolted toward the front door. She heard Clover barking frantically from the other side. Steve had his gun at the ready just in case there was someone else in the house.

Thankfully, that was not the case.

"It's all clear. Is the safe still here?"

Willow's bedroom was a disaster. "I didn't leave it like this, I promise." Drawers were open and all her underclothing was upset. The thought of someone rummaging through her personal things gave her the heebie jeebies. She shuddered.

She had placed the small locked safe at the back of her walk in closet. She prayed it was still there. She sighed a breath of relief when she reached the back of her closet and found it in one of the mostly unused suitcases stacked together. "It's still here." She called out to Steve.

She set the safe on her bed then opened it. "Here you go. It's all yours." She handed him the note that accompanied the manuscript.

"He barely knew you, right? Why would he send this to you? It makes no sense."

"Perhaps he figured no one would suspect me having the manuscript. And just maybe his agent would get it before anyone did figure it out."

"If, and that is a big if, that was the thought behind it, well, it didn't quite work out the way he intended, did it? Now you have a murderer attached to you for something that doesn't really concern you. He put you in harm's way without giving a thought to your wellbeing nor considering your wishes. In some ways, I wish the guy would have found the darn safe and taken the manuscript. At least then he would have what he wants and most likely you would be out of danger."

Willow smiled. *He does care.* "I'm sure I'll be fine. I have Clover and my handy Taser. I'm also going shopping for my hand gun. Want to go with?"

Steve's eyes brightened. "Yeah. I can help you pick something out. If you want me to, that is."

"Of course. That is why I asked. You'd know better than me what to get."

The police officers who had finished examining the ice cream shop were now parked outside her home.

She looked up at him. "Did you ever get into his laptop? Find out if the manuscript is on there?"

He nodded his head. "Yeah, he had his passwords written down on a small slip of paper underneath his desk calendar. And no, no sign of the manuscript. I spoke with his agent and she was surprised he had anything for her. Apparently, the last couple of his books were written by ghost writers. He was having something of a writer's block."

Willow was surprised. "He was frantically working on something on that laptop of his. I wonder what it was."

"Our tech guy didn't find anything. Nothing at all."

Willow thought back to the last time she had seen him writing. "Did they check the flash drive? He always used one to store his work."

Steve shook his head. "I don't know. I wasn't aware there was a flash drive. I'll have to see if one was catalogued with the evidence. Although I'm sure if there was, I would have known about it."

"Huh. I'm sure he had it with him the night before the festival." She paused. "Steve, I think the murderer took the flash drive when they ambushed Rune. And I'm pretty certain that is what this is all about. Huxley Rune stole someone's manuscript. He was going to pass it off as his own and that person doesn't relish the idea of handing their work over to him. The question is, who is it?"

She added, "I think this rules out Gloria, don't you? I mean, she had the bits and pieces of burnt manuscript tacked to her wall of shame. She wouldn't have done that if she had written the book. She may be a stalker, but I don't think she's a murderer."

"I think you're right. Maybe my guys will turn up a fingerprint or some DNA. If we get some firm evidence, we can wrap this thing up and perhaps keep you out of trouble." He narrowed his eyes. "Which you seem to be very good at getting into."

"My mom used to call me 'Willow Nothing But Trouble Crier.' So, I guess she was right." She smiled. "I managed to get into a lot of trouble back then too. Although I'm not sure stealing cookies from the cookie jar and pies from the window sill prepared me for my life of crime solving. Then again, who knows? We were old school. Mom would make me cut my own switch to whip my butt with. I think that is what turned me from the dark side. A good whipping."

As Willow walked back to the truck with Steve, he went down. "Darn it. What the heck?" His foot was shin high in a hole.

"Oh gosh. Another thing I forgot about. Clover seems to be bent on digging as many holes as she possibly can. What can I do to stop her? Just this week, I've fallen in two myself." She offered to take the safe with the manuscript still in it from him and he waved her off.

Steve mumbled under his breath as he hobbled to the truck then replied, "Let me ask my sister. She's bound to know with all the dogs they have." He deposited the safe safely in the back seat then drove to town.

Chapter 10

Willow entered the shop to find Embry pacing.

"You could have taken me with you. Mom, I was scared to death something was going to happen to you." She threw herself into her mother's arms and cried on her shoulder. "You're all I've got. You can't get hurt."

"Oh, Embry. I'm so sorry. I was so concerned about the manuscript and hopefully catching someone in the act, I didn't think. Again. Apparently that has become habit with me."

"Well? Did you catch em?"

"No, by the time we saw him he was on the outskirts of the woods. There was no hope in catching him at that point."

She poured herself a cup of coffee. "My head is killing me. Lack of caffeine, I'm sure." She cooled it down with a little cream then took a big sip and sighed. "Looks like the groupies have thinned out a bit." A smaller crowd was congregated at the front entrance, waiting for the coffee shop to open. Willow turned to her daughter. "You ready? Janie won't be here until after lunch. She broke a tooth. It's just me and you until then."

Embry tied her ice cream apron around her neck. "We can do this." She glanced at her watch. "We got a break. Nearly two hours off the time clock with the police doing their thing. I'll tell you one thing, these groupies sure are committed. It is hot out there!"

Willow unlocked the door. A couple of reporters as well as the groupies pushed their way in. It was going to be a long day, again. Perhaps she would have the money to have that book shelf made after all.

Janie and one of her part timers came in after lunch, which gave Willow and Embry a chance to sit and rest. Not to mention eat something. They took up residence in the office since there wasn't a table or chair to be had in the dining area. Steve popped his head in.

"You have room for one more?"

Willow patted a small wooden chest. "Will this do?" She started to rise and get him a snack and he stopped her.

"You look exhausted. I know how to pour coffee and cut banana bread. I'll be right back."

She wanted to tell him to eat one of the new fiber muffins but she didn't bother. Let him have the banana bread. Who was she kidding? She looked down at her cinnamon roll oozing with butter and smiled. Perhaps they would both get back to eating healthy tomorrow. Today, she was enjoying what was in front of her.

He returned with his banana bread sandwich.

"I see you found the peanut butter." She looked a little closer. "And the bananas." She nodded. "Clever. Maybe that should go on the menu."

He took a bite and closed his eyes, his pleasure obvious as he chewed then swallowed. "I imagine heaven will be like peanut butter banana bread sandwiches." He took a drink of his coffee then took another bite and groaned.

He finished the last crumb on his plate before he got around to what he wanted to tell her. Embry had already returned to the counter to help out so Willow was his one and only captivated audience member.

"Okay, we finished running Rune's financials. At first I figured his meager living conditions for either simplicity or humility. Turns out, the guy was nearly broke. And get this, he'd been paying out regular payments every month of ten thousand to some rehabilitation ranch out here in Oklahoma. That started 8 years ago and has been going on ever since. Another irregularity was sporadic payments ranging from 25 thousand to 100 thousand dollars being withdrawn in cash. To the tune of 350 thousand dollars being doled out. That is a lot of cash. It started shortly after the payments to the rehabilitation ranch started. The two have to be connected." He finished the last bit of his coffee. "Do you want to go with?"

"Are you kidding? Of course." She bit her bottom lip. "I'm supposed to have dinner with Embry tonight. How far away is this ranch?"

"Just a couple of hours. I'll have you back in time for an 8'o'clock supper. Promise."

"All right, let me go tell her what is going on. She is working till 8 anyway, so I'm sure she'll be fine with it."

Steve filled a couple of to-go cups with coffee while Willow chatted with Embry. They both could use the extra caffeine.

Willow took a sip of her coffee. "Perfect."

"It's hard to mess up coffee with a little cream."

"The polite thing to do is say thank you when someone pays you a compliment."

"Okay, thank you."

"He was being blackmailed. But why?"

"You don't beat around any bushes, do you? And yeah, that is what I was kinda figuring too. At any rate, we're about to find out. I could speculate, but that wouldn't do us a bit of good."

"True." She decided they both needed a break from shop talk. "How is your ankle?"

"Much better. I'll give my sister a call tonight and see what she suggests. There has to be something we can do. Someone is bound to get hurt."

She shook her head. "I love having her. I think we both need to go get some training."

"Good idea. The right training will make a world of difference."

Most of the trip was spent in a comfortable silence. Willow even caught herself falling asleep. His choice of soft instrumental music surprised her. She expected some twangy country and western, or perhaps gospel. But instrumental? Never. The music along with the warm sun relaxed her and she found her eyelids growing heavy. She startled awake and glanced over and noticed Steve had a grin on his face.

"What did I do?"

"Nothing."

"Obviously I did something. What was it?"

"Okay. I'll tell you. But don't get embarrassed."

She inwardly groaned. "Okay, I won't."

"When you're falling asleep you blow air through your lips, and it sort of sounds like a horse."

"You mean I snore?"

"Nope, it really sounds like a horse fluttering his lips. I don't know how else to explain it. But you do it perfectly. That is what woke you up."

"Huh." She wiped the drool from the side of her face. She hoped he didn't see that. A drooling horse. How attractive. "Sorry I fell asleep. I guess I'm just worn out. Someone kept me up too late last night."

"Hey, I had you home by 9:30. That's not late. Not by anyone's standards. Especially yours."

"I know. It's just been a long few days." She looked at the passing landscape. For a long time she missed the northern terrain and the seasons. She had come to appreciate the stark and sometimes bare Oklahoma land. It had a different kind of beauty. A raw beauty.

Steve slowed down and turned into a gated drive. The property was so large, Willow couldn't see the house from the road. After driving for nearly a mile, they pulled up in front of a large ranch. There wasn't a sign advertising what the place was. Nor was there any of the obvious telltale signs screaming, I'm a rehabilitation center.

In fact, Steve wasn't entirely sure he had the right place.

Together they approached the front door, hoping they would find the answers they needed.

Steve used the big brass knocker to announce their visit then waited. Willow raised her eyebrows but said nothing. He was about to knock again when the door slowly opened.

A tall stately woman with quick eyes and graceful movements opened the door. "Hello. How can I help you?" She was distinctly missing a southern accent.

"Hello, Ma'am. I'm looking for the Reed Rehabilitation Center." He flashed her his badge. "I would appreciate any help you can give."

She opened the door. "Come in. May I ask the reason behind your visit?"

"I'm not at liberty to say. I can tell you it is police business."

She directed them to sit in a small parlor near the entrance. "I will be right back. Please excuse me."

She disappeared down the hallway. A few minutes later voices could be heard approaching. One being the woman the other a male voice.

Both Steve and Willow stood as the couple neared them.

The gentleman motioned for them to sit back down then offered his hand. "I'm Mark Reed and this is my wife, Elizabeth. And you have found the Reed Rehabilitation Center. What can we help you with?"

Elizabeth was seated next to her husband and offered both Steve and Willow a welcoming smile.

Steve explained the situation, leaving out the possible blackmail payments, then waited for a response.

Elizabeth placed her hand on her husband's knee and nodded.

Mark responded. "We are very private. Not many people in the area know what we do. We have 12 guests in our home. All of them have been in some sort of debilitating accident. One fell in a mountain climbing accident. Another in a diving accident. The young lady you want information about was involved in an automobile accident. She is paralyzed from the neck down. She was struck by a drunk driver while riding her bicycle. The driver was Huxley Rune." He looked to his wife. "That was nearly eight years ago now, wasn't it?"

Elizabeth nodded then picked up where her husband left off. "Mr. Rune has been paying for Clarissa's care ever since. He even moved here a few years ago to be close to her. He visits every week and provides her with the best of everything to make her as comfortable as possible. When she was released from the hospital, her family wanted her here to be close to them. She was a student out east when this happened. Unfortunately, because of the extent of her injuries, she wasn't able to live at home. She needs round the clock care. That's where we come in."

"Because of what we do, our services do not come cheap. We have a full time medical staff as well as household staff that have to be paid. Nor can we accept everyone. We simply do not have the room."

A woman bearing a tray appeared and Elizabeth stood to help. "It's a long drive from the city. Please, help yourselves. You must be in need of refreshments."

There was a carafe of aromatic coffee, hot water with various tea bags, both savory and sweet Kolaches, and a lovely pitcher of water with sliced fruit mixed in.

Mark smiled. "I'm not shy." He placed a few pieces of the succulent pastry on his plate then poured himself a cup of coffee.

Steve followed suit. He could eat anywhere, anytime. Willow was sure of it.

Elizabeth handed her a small delicate plate with pink roses painted along the edge. "Please, have some."

Steve asked the question that was plaguing both him and Willow. "What will happen to Clarissa now that Mr. Rune has passed away?"

"She'll be fine. The last time he visited, he brought us a copy of his will. He seemed to be upset, but wouldn't tell us what was bothering him. Clarissa is the sole beneficiary of Mr. Rune's estate."

Steve sighed. "I hate to tell you this, but Mr. Rune was nearly broke when he died. He has nothing left."

Mark chuckled. "Huxley Rune was a master at making money. I can assure you, he wasn't broke. He may not have had much in his bank accounts, but the man was worth millions. Would you like to see a copy of his will?"

Steve's eyes brightened. "Yes, we have been trying to locate his lawyer. With no luck, I might add. His agent promised to have him get in touch with me and I'm still waiting."

Mark left then returned with a manila file and handed it to Steve. "You can have that one. I made you a copy."

Steve stood up. "Thank you. There is one more thing." He seemed hesitant but asked anyway. "Do you know of anyone who wanted to use this information against him? We believe he may have been being blackmailed."

Mark took his wife's hand in his own. "The whole ordeal was very hush-hush. Not even the papers caught wind that Mr. Rune was involved in the accident. Huxley Rune was a very protected man. He had friends in high places. To my knowledge, he never again touched a drop of alcohol. I have no idea who may have found out. We have kept our end of the deal. Until today, we have told no one."

Elizabeth added. "Clarissa's family was thankful he did the right thing by coming to them. He had his lawyers draw up papers that made him legally responsible for her care, for the rest of her life. Since all his assets were responsible for the wonderful care she is receiving, her mother never had cause to sue him. Not many people know about this arrangement. I can't imagine her mother blackmailing him. She's one of his biggest fans."

Willow spoke for the first time. "Who is Clarissa's mother?"

"Martha Claremont. Do you know her?"

Willow swallowed hard. "Yes, yes we do."

Chapter 11

"How did I not know Martha had a daughter?"

Steve shrugged his shoulders. "Most of us know she has a daughter. She led us all to believe her daughter was still out east working in a cushy job earning lots of money. We had no idea her daughter was in a debilitating accident and living two hours from home. None whatsoever. Some of us did wonder why she never visited, but we didn't think it was our place to ask."

"I would think something like this would have gotten out somehow. The gossip alone in a small town can be brutal. Someone had to have known."

"If so, they must have a tongue of steel because I haven't heard a word about it." He sighed. "This does mean we have to talk to Martha. Hopefully we can keep it quiet. For some reason she doesn't want people to know and I'd like to try and honor her wishes if at all possible."

Willow nodded. If Embry were in Clarissa's place, Willow would be devastated. Honoring Martha's wishes was the least they could do.

Willow opened the will and whistled. "Mark was right. He may not have much in his bank accounts but he has a lot elsewhere. Real estate, movie options, book royalties, he even has Xbox games based on his books."

"This is why we needed to talk to his lawyer. We just didn't have all the information we needed to be able to search his name accurately. I hate when lawyers impede an investigation."

Willow kept reading. "Oh wow. He already had most of his assets transferred to Clarissa. He was living bare bones by choice." She looked at Steve. "This still doesn't tell us where the $350,000 went. We need more information."

True to his word, Steve pulled up in front of Willow's Ice Cream Shoppe just before 8pm. She waved goodbye then went in through the back door.

The place was empty. Embry and her co-worker had already cleaned and mopped. Janie was her morning baker and would have the shelves filled by the time their morning regulars appeared.

"Okay, Mom, we have a reservation for 9. We need to get moving."

"Willow ran a brush through her hair and topped off her jeans and white t-shirt with a plaid jacket she kept around the office for good measure." She turned to Embry. "Do I look okay or do we need to stop at my house so I can change?"

"You're fine. I, however, have to change. I smell like rocky road, mint chocolate chip, and mocha lattes all rolled up in one. If we leave now, we'll have time to swing by my place and still make it."

Willow followed Embry to the city. No sense in making the girl drive her home. Not when she was working the breakfast shift at the restaurant the next morning.

Willow followed Embry to her apartment. The place was a disaster. "How do you find anything in here?"

"I have a unique organizational system. As long as you don't touch anything, I know right where everything is." Two minutes later, Embry emerged. "Do you see my tan sandals anywhere?"

Willow gave her a shake of the head and started looking under piles. She held up the AWOL sandals. "Are these the ones?"

"Ah yes, now I remember. I had them on then decided to wear heels and kicked them off."

"Good thing you have that wonderful system in place or you may never have found them."

Embry pursed her lips but didn't comment. Instead, she quickly put the sandals on. "Okay, let's go. You can leave your truck here if you want to."

"Uh, maybe you should leave your car here."

Embry smiled. "Good idea."

Willow drove the short distance to the downtown restaurant. She'd never been to the fine dining establishment but she already knew the food was delicious. Embry had brought her bits and pieces of leftovers over the months she had worked there.

The waitress appeared and seemed genuinely pleased to see her daughter. "Embry, is this your mom?"

Embry made introductions then ordered an appetizer for the both of them and a glass of wine for herself.

"And for you ma'am?"

Willow was looking at the menu so she half mumbled, "I'll have a half and half ice tea."

"Did you say an Arnold Palmer?"

Willow laughed. "Oh, goodness no. I'd be under the table. I'll have a half sweet and half unsweet ice tea."

The waitress gave her an odd look then told her the tea would be unsweetened with simple syrup on the side then left to get their drinks.

Embry started laughing. "Mom, what is an Arnold Palmer?"

"I suppose it's some sort of alcohol. Probably a whisky or something."

This made Embry laugh even harder. "Mom, an Arnold Palmer is half ice tea, half lemonade. It doesn't have any alcohol it in."

"Oh. Wonder why they call it that? Wouldn't it be easier if they just said what it was?"

The waitress brought their drinks and Willow started to explain but Embry kicked her under the table.

"Ow. What'd you do that for?"

Embry addressed her co-worker. "I'm ordering for both of us. Mom will have the Chilean Sea Bass and I'll have the Colorado Lamb Chop."

Willow was still rubbing her shin when the waitress collected their menus and left. "That better have been an accident." Their charcuterie board was placed before them. "I could have ordered a hamburger. It would have saved you some money."

"Mom, stop trying to save me money. I work. I save. I'm buying you a nice dinner now would you just stop and enjoy it?"

"Sheesh. Okay. Fine." She mumbled under her breath.

"What did you say?"

"Nothing."

"That's what I thought. Now, eat some cheese and meat."

They took their time and enjoyed one another's company. Willow had been so busy with the ice cream festival, they didn't have much leisure time. Work, yes, but not play time. Willow thought back to the day of revelations regarding Martha's daughter, Clarissa. As she looked at her own daughter, laughing and telling her something about one of the waiters, she felt her eyes tear up. She now understood Martha a little better. She was so quiet and didn't seem to get out much. She did get out and she did spend time with her daughter, just not in the way she would have liked.

Willow blinked away the tears. She wanted to enjoy these moments with her daughter, not be a downer for both of them.

Their entrees came and as usual, they traded plates halfway through the meal. By the time their chocolate torte and coffee arrived both of them were plumb stuffed. Willow wouldn't trade her time with her daughter for anything. Nor would she stop at anything to protect her. The owners of the rehabilitation center said Martha had nothing to gain by suing, but, Willow wondered. If she knew her daughter would be taken care of, and there would be no end to the money, would she take matters into her own hands and exact revenge?

Chapter 12

The alarm went off before Willow was ready. Clover was snoring next to her. She must have let her out at some point, not that she remembered, then fell back into bed in her near zombie state. She called Janie to see if the groupies were still hanging out.

Janie assured her they were fine and she didn't need to come in at all. Just stay home and rest was the order from her best friend. She didn't argue. She went straight back to bed, pulled the covers over her head and promptly started snoring. Her phone was turned off. Not even on vibrate, but turned off. She wanted no interruptions. She wanted to sleep until she woke up.

The sun was high in the sky when she finally turned over and stretched. Apparently Clover had the same idea as she barely acknowledged her as she reached for the fur ball sleeping next to her. In fact, Clover got a bit irritated and moved to the other side of the bed when her sleep was disturbed. Willow laughed. "I know how you feel, girl. We are kindred spirits in that sense."

Willow flipped the coffee maker on and opened her laptop. She hadn't checked email in days and Facebook probably thought she had passed away. She had removed the app from her phone. Email too. She hated the constant pinging. Whatever was happening could live without her until she was actually sitting in front of her computer.

"Huh, Clover, what do you think about that? A Russian girl is wanting to hook up with me. Yeah, I don't think so." She pressed the delete button. So much trash. A couple emails from friends and a sale for her favorite face cream. She clicked on the link and was about to order when an instant message popped up. "Mom, trying to call you. Why isn't your phone on?"

Willow rolled her eyes. "I guess it's time to reconnect." She pulled her phone from her purse and turned it on. She had multiple missed calls and several voice mails, two from Embry, one from Steve, and one from Janie. The rest of the missed calls were hang ups.

She closed down her laptop and called Embry. "Yes? You rang?"

"Mom, gosh, where have you been all day? I've been trying to reach you."

"I've been here. Sleeping. See, that is why my phone was off. So I could sleep."

"But, what if there was an emergency or someone died."

"Embry, what do you want?"

"Oh, can I borrow your pink sweater? The one you bought when we were shopping this spring?"

"That was the emergency? I'm so glad my phone was off and yes, you may borrow my sweater. The important word to remember is borrow. I want it back."

"Great. I'll be over later to get it. I've got a date tomorrow night and it will be perfect. See you later. Love you."

Willow hung up the phone after telling her daughter she loved her too.

Steve was next.

"Hey, you called?"

"I sure did. I went to see Martha this morning."

This got Willow's attention. "Without me?"

"I tried to call but you weren't answering. I had to get some answers."

"I was so tired I collapsed. Well, what did she say?"

"Pretty much what Mark and Elizabeth said. She didn't give much more insight or reveal anything we didn't already know. I did get the distinct impression she is hiding something though. And she definitely wants us to remain quiet about the whole incident. She does not want people knowing Clarissa was involved in the accident or that she lives here in the vicinity."

"Huh, I wonder why?"

"I have no idea. I need to get going. I'm glad you got the chance to rest. I'm looking forward to the same thing one of these days." He paused, "I almost forgot. I talked with my sister. She wants to know how much you are actually playing with Clover. Going on walks, throwing a ball, that sort of stuff. Apparently dogs dig holes when they're bored."

"I guess not as much as I should be. I'll try and increase our together time."

She hung up and spent the next hour and a half cleaning her house. Both bathrooms were horrendous. And dog hair was everywhere. She emptied the vacuum bag before putting it away then scratched Clover behind the ear. "Do you want to go for a walk?" Clover ran to the door and barked. "I'll take that as a yes." She spent the next hour walking and throwing Clover's ball.

As they approached the house, Embry pulled up. She rolled down the window.

"Hey, Mom. You and Clover out getting into trouble?"

Willow waved. "You know it."

Clover flopped down on the cool floor after taking a nice long drink.

"That should keep her from digging any more holes."

Willow was still restless. She had put supper in the crockpot when she got up so she checked on it and found it was ready. Which was a good thing, since she'd worked up quite the appetite. She mixed in the parmesan cheese and set the table while it melted. Willow paced as Embry searched her closet for the pink sweater.

"You hungry?" She called down the hall.

"I'm always hungry. What'd you make?"

"I have farro risotto in the crockpot with chicken and mushrooms, a Caesar salad, and some rolls. Interested?"

Embry stuck her head out Willow's bedroom door. "You know I am."

"Okay, well, it's ready. Come and eat."

Half way through the meal, Embry interrupted Willow's thoughts. "Mom, you're so quiet. What is up?"

She told her about Martha and Clarissa, making sure she knew it was not to be repeated. "I just can't seem to get what happened out of my head. I think I'm going to go by there after you go."

Embry ate then rushed out the door. "Thanks for the meal and the sweater."

Willow watched as Embry's car blew up dust leaving the driveway then she took a quick shower. She was still sweaty from cleaning and her walk with Clover. She put her wet hair in a low bun, slipped on a pair of capris and a t-shirt then headed to her truck. As Willow reached the end of her driveway, a car was slowly approaching. As soon as the driver noticed Willow, he sped up. Willow waved and the driver pretended not to see her.

"Hmm, I wonder what Jasper James is doing in this neck of the woods."

Chapter 13

Willow parked on the street in front of Martha's house. All the drapes were pulled and she didn't want to be visiting too late. She glanced at the time. It was only 7 pm. Not too late, at least in her eyes.

She rang the doorbell and waited. She rang it again. Still no answer. Willow walked around to the back of the house to see if she might be sitting outside enjoying some fresh air. Nope. It was then she saw the garden and one leg protruding from the tomato plants. She pulled out her phone while running toward Martha.

"Martha, are you okay?"

Willow dialed 911 as she checked for a pulse and open airways. She gave the dispatcher the address then attended to Martha. Thankfully she was breathing. It was only a couple of minutes before she heard the ambulance. The EMT's loaded her into the ambulance and left with their lights blaring. The only thing Willow knew when they left was she was breathing on her own but she was unresponsive. She let herself in the back door of the house justifying her behavior by telling herself she was only checking to make sure nothing was in or on the stove and if there were animals, she would check on them. The woman did like to drink tea. It was entirely possible she had a tea kettle going.

She was in the bedroom when she heard someone else in the house. She looked around for a place to hide when a familiar deep voice called out to her.

"Willow, I know you're in here."

She grinned. "I was checking to make sure she didn't leave the stove on."

"In the bedroom?"

"Um, yeah, some people have coffee machines in their bedrooms."

Steve leaned against the door frame. "And did Ms. Claremont have a tea pot going in her bedroom?"

"No, no she did not. You can never be too sure though."

"Let me ask this. Did you find anything useful?"

"I'm not sure. She has this envelope of letters she wrote to the Times and various other newspapers in the northeast. Asking all of them why they haven't reported on the hit and run. And yes, apparently, Mr. Rune did not develop a conscious and turn himself in until a few weeks after the accident. I would say he had a major change of heart with leaving Clarissa everything in his will." She glanced at Steve. "Mark and Elizabeth left out that part of the story." She sighed. "Then again, perhaps they had no idea. Maybe Huxley didn't give them the full story, you know, perhaps he kept the not so flattering parts to himself."

"I doubt they had any reason to withhold that information if they knew of it. How would it benefit them? The accident was years ago and Rune is dead. He is beyond facing the consequences."

"Yeah, very true. Did you know one of his books was just optioned for movie rights?" Willow thought about the girl whose life was terribly altered. "She has all this money and can't enjoy it." She had an idea. "Steve, who is acting as the trustee for Clarissa?"

He rolled his eyes. "We're still waiting on the lawyer. I have a phone meeting with him tomorrow morning at 9 am. I should get some answers then."

"Well, let's hope he comes through."

"Yeah, let's hope so. This guy is slippery."

She frowned. "I'm going to go by the hospital to check on Martha. Do you want to come?"

He nodded. "What, with you driving? I'd be putting my life in my own hands. How about I drive. At least I know I'll make it there and back in one piece." He added, "Besides, you won't get much information since you aren't family. But, I'm guessing you already knew that, didn't you?"

She started toward the front door. "I'll never tell." She smiled as she skipped down the stairs, Steve close on her heels. She held up her keys. "Come on, live a little."

"Fine. You drive. I'll pray."

She laughed.

By the time they reached the hospital the hallways were dimmed and most of the patients were already given their medications. Steve had been correct, Willow had to wait in the waiting room while he discussed Martha's condition. Thankfully her attending physician spoke a little louder than necessary and she got most of what he was saying. She wasn't certain if that was for her benefit or if he was just a natural loud mouth. Whichever was the case, she was thankful.

On their way out, she discussed the results with Steve. "So, she had been drugged. Steve, this is much bigger than a manuscript. Although I'm sure people have been killed for less. I have a feeling this has a lot to do with a whole lot of money. Plain old fashioned greed."

It was midnight before Willow unlocked her front door. The mess that greeted her shouldn't have been a surprise, then again, whoever was looking for that manuscript didn't know that Steve took it to the police station. She called him.

"Our visitor has been here again."

"Where is that guard dog of yours?"

She opened the utility room door and there was clover, licking a large red dog toy that had been stuffed with peanut butter. "You'll have to see it to believe it."

"I'm on my way."

Fifteen minutes later, Steve was standing next to Willow, also watching the dog lick peanut butter. "Looks like we have someone who has intimate knowledge of dogs on our hands." He looked around the room. "It's not too bad. The last time we processed the scene we didn't find one questionable finger print. Looks like things are out of place, but nothing looks broken or damaged on purpose."

She had to agree. Her intruder was being very careful with her things. She was thankful for that. "Just go home and get some rest. I'll clean up here in the morning. It's all good. Besides, I have a good idea who is looking for that manuscript."

"Are you going to share?"

"If I'm right, and I believe I am, then I'm not in any danger. I'll let you know afterward and you can decide if you need to intervene."

He had learned to trust her judgement, even if her methods were a little questionable. "Okay, but only if you're sure."

She stood staring at him, the moonlight softening the landscape behind him in the doorway. "I'm sure." She sighed.

He reached up and brushed her bangs off her forehead. "I'll be talking to you tomorrow then."

"Till tomorrow."

Chapter 14

The next morning Clyde was sitting outside the coffee shop, waiting for his morning cup of hot cocoa. "Hello, Ms. Willow."

"Hello, Clyde. How are you today?" He always waited on her to come. She wasn't sure why. Janie was already on the premises and serving up the early birds.

"I'm good. Mama told me to hurry up today. We have to go shopping for her new…" He leaned in and whispered. "…underwear." Just saying the word made him laugh. He opened the door and waited for her before he followed behind. When he calmed down he said, "She said we might as well get me some new pants. My stomach is getting too big for my other pants. I have to wear exercise pants even though I don't exercise much."

"Do you think you need to give up your morning hot cocoa?"

"Why would I need to do that?"

"Oh, never mind, Clyde. I'll make your hot cocoa in just a minute, okay?"

"Okay. Did you catch the lady who killed Mr. Rune? Mama said she didn't kill Mr. Rune. Somebody stole her underwear. They pretended to be mama so the police wouldn't know who really did it. That's what mama said."

Willow tilted her head in thought then shook it off. Clyde wasn't a credible witness. He had no idea what he had seen or what he didn't see. Getting information from him was like putting a puzzle together. In his mind, it all worked. To anyone on the outside looking in, the pieces were jumbled together haphazardly and they made no sense whatsoever.

She made him his cocoa and sent him on his way.

Janie handed her a cookie. "Here, have one. It's your peanut butter cookies."

"Our customers will be happy today. These things melt on the tongue." Willow poured herself a cup of coffee, added her cream, and then took a bite of the delicious baked good.

"Well, have you figured out who killed Mr. Rune?"

"I'm getting there. An idea is starting to form, it just needs to clear up. Still fuzzy around the edges. Martha would never have given herself too much potassium. Only the killer would have done that. Which of course clears Martha.

Apparently if I had waited to go talk to her she would have been dead by the time we found her. Talk about perfect timing."

"I would say so. I think it might be the only time I would consider myself lucky to be considered a murder suspect."

"Tell me about it. She has a lot of UTI's and drinks a lot of cranberry juice. Someone spiked it with a huge dose of potassium. Whoever tried to kill her knows her well enough to know her health conditions."

"That narrows it down."

"Not enough though. It could still be anyone. Even her neighbors or friends." She took another sip of the hot liquid. "No, this is someone altogether different. Someone who has something to gain by her death."

Willow waited for Steve to either come in or call her after his morning phone appointment but she didn't hear from him. Finally, after lunch he stopped in.

"Hey, there you are. What happened, did you talk with the lawyer?"

He smirked. "No, he postponed. Apparently he got called into court and there was nothing he could do. He is supposed to call me tomorrow morning. I stressed to his secretary how important it is we speak. She assured me he understands." He shrugged his shoulders. "Not much I can do. At least not yet. If this goes on too much longer I'll fly out there and show up with the local police. That should get his attention."

"I hope it doesn't come to that. How inconvenient can it be to pick up a phone and make a five minute phone call? Certainly he has a spare five minutes, doesn't he?"

"I would think so." He held up his thermal coffee cup. "Can I get that cup of coffee now?"

She leaned on the counter. "I don't seem to recall, did you ever make it into that dunk tank?"

He took out his wallet and put a buck on the counter. "I'm paying, sheesh."

She giggled and pushed his dollar back to him. "I have a thing for police officers, remember?"

Chapter 15

By the time Willow locked up the shop it was after 9 pm. She wondered how her daughter's date was going then made a mental note to call her the next day. Unfortunately, her daughter was busy so she was going to have to carry out her plan on her own. As much as she would have liked to have a partner in crime, one wasn't to be found. Janie was exhausted when she left that afternoon so she didn't bother asking her to be an accomplice. She squared her shoulders. "I can do this on my own."

It was already getting dark. Willow was grateful. Darkness would help her accomplish her task without being seen. She drove about 20 miles and parked on a side street, a block away from the house she wished to visit. Spy on was probably the correct term. She pretended to be on a leisurely stroll, simply someone out enjoying the cooler evening weather.

Finally she reached her destination. She looked up and down the street, making sure no one was looking, and then she ducked into the side yard. She had her mini flash light on her key chain to help light her path.

A light was shining from an open window facing the back yard. A neighbor's dog barked and made her jump. Thank goodness the dog was fenced in. She crouched down and slowly rose up to look in the window. Vick was busy applying, what looked like varnish, to a set of bookshelves. She wasn't sure why she didn't just knock on the door and ask him why he lied to her, but she thought perhaps he had something else to hide. Like a typewriter and a thesaurus. Maybe he had asked Rune to look over his manuscript he had been toiling over for years and Rune stole it. She scooted down onto the ground and leaned her back against the brick. What was she missing?

She crossed the back yard to the west side of the house and looked in the other window. "I knew it. I just knew it." There, sitting on a desk was an old fashioned typewriter. Just like the one used to type the paper manuscript Chief Grice now had in his possession at the police station. She had just came out from around the back of the house when a policeman yelled at her to stop where she was at.

She stopped and raised her hands. Her eyes were wide with surprise.

He began to approach and she started to move and he pulled his Taser out. "Ma'am, I'll say it again. Stand where you are with your arms up over your head. Do not make any sudden moves." Once again he began to walk toward her. This time she stayed completely still.

"Ma'am, we had a neighbor call reporting a peeping Tom. Well, I guess in your case it would be a peeping Ann." He laughed at his own joke.

Willow didn't respond. "I'm not a peeping Tom, or Ann for that matter. I'm on a case."

He took a step back. "Are you an officer? You should have identified yourself."

"Well, not really."

"You either are or aren't."

"Okay, I'm not. But, I'm still on a case. Maybe you heard of me. I'm Willow Crier. I'm the one who figured out who murdered that food critic a few weeks ago."

"Oh, yeah, I remember that case…"

He was interrupted by Vick who was now trying to figure out what was happening outside his house.

"Willow, is that you?"

"Yes, it's me." She followed Vick as he limped across the lawn.

"Looks like you have a sprained ankle there, Vick."

He quickly looked up. "Officer, it's okay. Willow wasn't trespassing. She is here to look at some bookshelves for her shop."

Willow was about to counter him but he put his hand up to stop her so she clamped her lips shut.

"She is here on my invitation. I'm sure she was just trying to get my attention. I was working in the back of the house."

The police officer turned to Willow. "Why didn't you just say that in the first place?"

He walked back to his squad car and yelled over his shoulder. "Next time don't be slinking around in the dark."

Willow turned to Vick. "So, you fell in one of my dog's holes when you were fleeing my house?"

He ran his hand through his hair. "Yeah, that was me. I'm sorry, okay? I was looking for my manuscript. I didn't know what else to do."

"Why didn't you just ask me for it?"

"Because, I didn't want anyone to think I murdered him. I didn't. I just wanted my book back."

"Why did you lie to me when I asked you if you knew Rune? I know you made his bookshelves. That was clearly your work."

His shoulders slumped. "First, I have a non-disclosure agreement with Rune. Most of the woodworking I do is for pretty famous people. They do not want their stories or pictures of their homes sold to the tabloids. It's happened more than once to a lot of them so they're pretty careful now. So legally I couldn't admit how I knew him. And second, when I learned he had been murdered I was trying to distance myself from him. I didn't think anyone would figure out I knew him."

"Tell me what happened."

"He commissioned me to make some book shelves. When I learned who he was, well, I asked him to look over a manuscript I had written. It took me years to write the thing and I almost threw it away. But, I thought, what if it's halfway decent? So, he finally agreed. I thought he would be a gentleman about the whole thing and give it back to me when he finished. Instead, he kept making excuses about why he hadn't read it yet. He was working so hard on his own manuscript, and on and on the excuses went. Finally, I asked him to just give it back to me. He refused. That is when I knew he never planned on giving it back. You can ask my lawyer. I've been in contact with him over the whole issue. If I was going to kill him, why would I have bothered with my lawyer?"

"Is the only reason you participated in the craft show to let Rune know you hadn't given up? I can't imagine you really wanting to sit out in the heat all day just to hand out business cards to us normal folks."

"Yeah, that about sums it up. I left him a message I'd be there and I wanted my manuscript back. He probably erased it as he didn't want anyone knowing the manuscript was mine."

"You know I'm going to have to report this, right?" She folded her arms. "And you are going to have to come over and help put my house together again. And I'm going to need a supply of peanut butter. My dog is addicted."

"I understand."

"And you're going to have to give me a pretty big discount when I order that set of bookshelves for the shop and you're going to have to have my truck cleaned. I'm assuming it was you who painted on my windshield and left ice cream to melt on my desk?"

"Done, done, and yes. Again, I'm sorry."

"All right. I forgive you. I do understand, you know. I can't imagine having my shop stolen out from under me. I just wish you would have come to me and been honest." She added for good measure. "If it's the same manuscript that Rune was supposed to be working on when he died, I have seen little bits and pieces. It's a good story. I hope you get somewhere with it."

He grinned. "That means a lot. Thank you."

Chapter 16

Willow glanced at the clock in her truck. It was after 11. She was thankful she wasn't sitting in a jail cell. It's the only thing that really caused her to show some leniency toward Vick.

She didn't care what time it was. She pulled in front of Jasper's house. *Every light in the house is on. What is he doing? He's probably just a night owl.* She rapped on his door, lightly at first then a bit harder.

He opened the door with a pencil behind his ear and a notebook in hand. "Hey, Willow. What are you doing out this time of night?" He walked back through the house so she closed the door and followed him. She really didn't think he murdered Rune but she had to check him off her list before she could move forward.

He led her to a room in the interior of the house with no windows. Everywhere she looked were pieces of body part furniture, like the leg lamp stand from The Christmas Story. *Creepy!*

"Um, Jasper, what is all this for?"

"Oh, this? I'm working on a book. I like to have as many tangible hands on props as I can get when I write. It makes it so much more real to me." He wiggled his eye brows. "Better for the story too. Makes it more real."

She was afraid to ask how body part furniture fit in with western stories, so she didn't. Instead she asked, "I saw you drive past my house the other day. I waved but when you saw it was me you sped up and didn't acknowledge me. Was there a reason?"

"Oh, pulling an Elaine from Seinfeld, huh? I like it. Let me write this one down. I love when I get ideas from unexpected places."

"Jasper, I'm being serious. I want to know."

He came closer. "Do you remember this one?" He stepped even closer and started throwing out lines from the show. "Do you remember it? The Close Talker? Elaine's boyfriend?"

Willow took a step back and tripped over the leg of the chair which caused Jasper to bust out laughing.

"That's exactly what Kramer did. I had no idea you loved that show as much as I do."

Willow stood up and brushed the seat of her pants off. "Jasper, what did you do on Thursday morning?"

"Oh, Thursday? I went to an estate sale out in the country." He held up his leg lamp. "It's where I got this beauty. Do you like it?"

She fired another question. "What is your favorite flavor of ice cream?"

"Pistachio. Are we playing 50 questions? Is it my turn? Are you a writer too? You must be because you totally get my sense of humor."

"Thanks, Jasper. I've gotta get home."

"Come around any time and we can practice more lines from Seinfeld. Man, I love that show. You know what, I think I need a break. I'm gonna watch a few episodes. I have the complete collection. Anytime you want to borrow it, just let me know." He turned and entered another room, closing the door behind him.

Willow turned in a circle taking in everything in the room. A remote control hand? A stool with buttocks carved into the seat? A mannequin lamp with a shade as its head? Weird. It was the only word she had. Okay, creepy still worked as well. That one was standing firm. She found the front door and let herself out.

Perhaps tomorrow Steve will get some answers.

Chapter 17

Willow was glad to be back to a normal schedule. She finally felt caught up on rest. She didn't have to report to the shop until after lunch so that gave her all morning to make phone calls, go to her hair dresser, and buy a new toy for Clover. If she had time, she would swing into the grocery store and pick up a few things. She was getting low on all the basics.

After calling to make an appointment and finding out her hairdresser was out of town, Willow searched the internet for another salon. *Hmmm, the Red Robin. I remember that name I just don't know where from.* She made an appointment.

Willow's hair was separated into small sections with half her scalp covered in a dark auburn solution when her phone rang. Too bad her regular stylist was out of town. She could have rescheduled and lived with a skunk stripe but she didn't have the patience for that. She was trying to nonchalantly look at the caller ID without appearing to be rude. She disliked rude people. She hated rude behavior. At that moment she was close to hating herself. Nothing bugged her more than someone in line at the checkout lane while jabbering on the phone. That was rude. If she could just turn her phone over and see who it was.

Her stylist interrupted her. "Do you need to get that?"

"Um, no. No, that's okay. It can wait."

The stylist waited for her to sit up straight. "Good, cause there is nothin' I hate more than somebody ignoring me when I'm workin' on their hair." She blew a bubble with the wad of gum she was chewing. "I'm glad you get that, girl."

All of a sudden, the girl started coughing. Willow felt a thump up against the back of her head. *No, please tell me she didn't. Please, no.* Willow reached around and felt the gum mixed with the dry portion of hair that had no solution.

"I almost choked. Ain't nobody come to my rescue. Did you see that? I had to give myself the Heimlich." She walked away for a minute then returned, with more gum in her mouth. "Now, I may have to cut your hair a little shorter. You'll look real nice with short hair."

Willow stood up and turned around. "I don't want you to touch my hair. Ever again. Do you hear me?"

The owner of the salon came running over. "Is there a problem here?"

Willow pointed to the wad of pink bubble gum in her hair. "What do you think? Do you think I have a problem?"

"Lola, you are finished here. Go back to the kitchen and get some ice. And spit that gum out while you're back there."

The young girl sulked and mumbled the entire way back to the stylist's lounge.

"I'm so sorry. I really thought she'd work out."

Willow wasn't going to be pacified. "What are we going to do here? Half my head is going to be dark auburn the other half is going to be short and streaked with grey. We need a plan before my hair starts falling out from the chemicals."

"Your hair isn't going to fall out, I promise. We're not going to let that happen." She took the ice cube from Lola and worked on freezing the gum. She slowly picked it from the tangles. "I'm going to have to rinse the hair that has already been dyed. Then I'll dye the other half. Again, I'm so sorry for all of this. It won't happen again."

At that very moment she remembered where she heard the name, Red Robin. Martha, whose hair was always longer on one side than the other. *You're darn right it won't happen again.* "What time is it?"

"12:30"

So much for my other errands. "I've got to go. Hurry up and rinse my hair." Janie had her second dentist appointment and Willow had to be there to relieve her. She had no choice in the matter. Gloria had called and said now that her heart throb was dead she was moving back out east. She wouldn't be back in. And her part timers weren't coming in until dinner time. She was all there was. Hair finished or not.

Willow drove as fast as she would allow herself. Embry and Steve would be proud. She pulled into the parking lot behind her shop at 12:55. *Just in time!*

She hurried into the building and Janie met her in the kitchen.

Janie stared and remained silent for at least thirty seconds. When she finally found her voice, she asked, "What happened to you?"

As Willow started explaining, Janie doubled over in laughter. "Willow, you're going to make me pee my pants. Oh my gosh. I would have rescheduled. Seriously, it would have been better than you coming to work like this."

"I was so mad I could have spit nails. I swear it. You should have seen her. And then she had the audacity to put more gum in her mouth. No, I'll get some dye and we'll do it ourselves. For now…" She tucked her hair up in a kerchief. "…this will work."

Janie's mouth dropped. She had no more words. Nothing.

"Well, will you help me later tonight?"

"Yes, I will. In fact, I'll stop by the beauty supply store and pick up what we need. Dark auburn, you say?"

"Yes, dark auburn."

"What time are you leaving here?"

"As soon as the girls get here. They can handle it for tonight."

"I'll be at your place at 6. Dinner and dye in hand."

The corner of Willow's lips turned downward.

Janie hugged her friend. "It's going to be okay. No one will probably even notice." Not that Janie believed a word of it. But, she had to encourage her friend somehow. "I'll see you in a little while."

After Janie left, Willow remembered the phone call she received at the salon. She dug her phone out of her purse. *Steve. He must have news.*

The dining area was quiet so she called him back and got his voicemail. "Hey, it's me. I'm at work, so give me a call when you get this."

She busied herself taking inventory. She was in the middle of counting her ice cream stock when the bell on the door jingled. "I'll be right there." She yelled from the back room.

She wrote down her final count then went to the counter to help the customer. Steve was standing in the dining area. He turned when he heard her approach.

"I got your..." He changed direction mid-sentence. "Your hair is two different colors."

She put her hand up. "Don't ask. Did you speak with the attorney?"

Steve was having a hard time not staring. He knew the smart thing would be to pretend everything was normal. He wasn't doing a good job of it. "Um, yes." His eyes kept drifting to her hair. She had put on a kerchief but it didn't do a very good job of covering her long tresses.

Willow was getting frustrated. "Well, what did he say?"

"What?"

"Did you hear a word I said? I asked what the lawyer said."

"Oh, yes, um, you're not going to believe who the trustee is."

She rolled her eyes. "Just tell me."

"It's her mother, Martha."

Chapter 18

Willow was sitting in her folding chair in her kitchen while Janie re-dyed her hair. "It can't be Martha. That just doesn't make sense. She would never overdose on Potassium. She just wouldn't do it. There has to be something I'm missing. She couldn't have guessed I would be along to save her. Nor would she try and kill herself. She has Clarissa to think about.

Janie began cooking dinner while Willow sat with the dye on her hair. "We are having comfort food tonight. If ever there was a day that called for it, it would be today."

"Mmm...sounds good. What are you making?"

"Tacos. Greasy, cheesy, spicy tacos. By the time you get out of the shower, they will be ready. Oh, with Guacamole on the side." She put the burger on to brown and started chopping vegetables.

Willow jumped in the shower when the timer went off and came out 20 minutes later to a buffet of taco fixings. Fresh guacamole included.

She loaded up her plate and sat down in front of the television. "Are we watching Downton Abbey?"

Janie had already taken a bite so she made a sound expressing her approval.

They either watched the show together or around the same time apart. It was their thing. That way they were always on the same episode and could rehash the whole show.

Willow brought out the ice cream after the first full episode. Two pints, butter pecan for Janie and double fudge brownie for herself. They both ate directly out of the carton. It was comfort food night. It was permissible.

Janie took a bite of ice cream then asked, "Who becomes the trustee if Martha dies?"

Willow stared at Janie. "You are right. You are 100% correct. Who does become trustee?" She had a pretty good idea.

Willow called Steve's cell phone. He sounded sleepy when he answered.

"Hey, it's me. Who becomes trustee if Martha dies?"

"I don't know. The lawyer is sending me a complete copy of the will. I should have it tomorrow. I guess we'll find out then."

Willow hung up. She didn't want to wait until tomorrow to find out. She looked at Janie. "Are you up for a little road trip?"

It was only 8 pm, not that late. Janie rubbed her eyes but agreed.

Willow pulled into the visitor parking at the hospital. Before leaving the shop, she had heard Martha was awake. They were able to steady her heart rate. Steve would probably go over in the morning to ask her what happened. Willow had a funny feeling they didn't have until morning.

She hurried into the hospital. Visiting hours were coming to a close so she said, "Just pretend you know exactly what you're doing. They won't bother you if they think you're supposed to be here."

Janie gave her friend a questioning look. "You've gotten sneaky."

"When you have had two people murdered under your nose and a third attempt, you have to be sneaky. It's the only way to survive."

She walked through the entrance with her shoulders squared and full of confidence. Janie followed her, looking a bit guiltier.

When they were safely in the elevator, Willow said, "You have to do better than that once we get to her floor or we'll never make it in. Perhaps you should act as a decoy."

[129]

"A decoy? What kind of decoy?"

"Oh, I don't know. Just ask where someone's room is."

"Whose?"

"Who cares? Just make up a name and be convincing. I'll need to slip by once you start asking questions at the nurses' station."

"Oh, how do I get myself into these things?"

Willow nodded. "You'll do fine. Just make something up."

Janie approached the nurses' station and asked where Mary Crawley's room was. Even Willow did a double take. *Really? You couldn't do better than that?*

The nurse questioned Janie. "Are you sure that is your friend's name?"

Willow snuck past the two of them without drawing any attention to herself. She rounded the corner and saw someone enter Martha's room. Someone who did not look like a nurse or doctor. She took off running. When she got to the room, a masked person had a pillow over Martha's face. Willow started yelling and the masked murdered pushed past her, into the hallway, and through the emergency exit doors. By the time Willow explained what she had seen the masked intruder had gotten away, or at least blended in with his surroundings.

Willow was still answering questions when Steve appeared.

"I should have known. What are you doing here?"

She feigned being offended. "And if I hadn't have come when I did, Martha would be dead. That is no way to thank me, now is it?"

"Once again, Willow to the rescue. Now, tell me what you're doing here."

"I had a funny feeling I needed to get up here, and fast. Something isn't right." She told him about her expeditions to check out Vick and Jasper and her conclusions regarding both of them.

"You know I'll have to question Vick, right?"

"Yeah, I told him as much. He is expecting you."

She followed Steve into Martha's room. "Are you okay?"

She nodded. "There was something about that man that was familiar. I couldn't see his face, but I recognized something about him." She looked to Willow and reached for her hand. "I hear I have you to thank for saving me."

Willow shook her head. "I just did what anyone would do. I wanted to talk to you. I thought perhaps you might have shared something with me you might have felt uncomfortable sharing with Police Chief Grice. I also wanted to let you know how sorry I was for the burden you've been carrying all this time by yourself."

"I've had help. I know I've kept Clarissa's accident quiet, but Rune ended up being a really good guy. He came to me a few weeks after the accident and accepted full responsibility. He apologized and even said he totally understood that I would probably never forgive him. He wouldn't forgive himself if he was in my shoes. I told him I was a good Christian woman and I have to forgive. I may not like it, but I would forgive him. Even if it took me a while to feel like forgiving him."

Steve asked the next question. "Do you remember anything about the day you collapsed? Was there anything out of the ordinary? Did you visit with anyone?"

"No, I did the same thing I do just about every day. I went to visit Clarissa then I came home to work in my garden. That was it. I didn't even have to go to the grocery store. Elizabeth was nice enough to send me home with a special cranberry cocktail to help with my, well, you know, female problems."

"I see. Did she do that often?"

"Oh, you know, now that I think about it, at least once a week. And it was helping. They are just the nicest people. They take such good care of my Clarissa. I'm not sure I could do it all by myself. They are such a blessing."

"Okay, you get some rest. We've stationed a police officer outside your door. You won't have any more problems like earlier, okay?"

She squeezed Steve's hand. "You two are both so wonderful. You make such a nice couple. Are you getting married soon?"

Steve's face turned a bright shade of crimson.

Willow responded. "Mrs. Claremont, we are just friends. Truly. But thank you for the compliment."

They left her alone to rest.

Steve took Willow's hand. "It really is a good thing you showed up here. Someone wants Martha out of the way."

"Yes, what we need to find out is, who benefits if Martha is no longer among the living? Call me as soon as you get the paperwork. I have a feeling I know exactly who benefits if Martha is gone."

He nodded. "Yeah, me too."

Chapter 19

Janie vowed to never again, as long as she lived, to go on another fact finding mission with Willow. "I lied to a nurse. A nurse."

"Well, technically you were asking a question."

"It was a lie, Willow."

"Speaking of which, did you really ask her if a character from Downton Abbey was a patient in the hospital? Couldn't you think of anyone else?"

"It was the first name that popped into my head. Okay? I'm not as good as you are at all this."

"Hmmm, well, it worked. So thank you. That is the important thing. And together, we saved Martha."

That made Janie smile. "It does feel good, doesn't it?"

"It sure does." Janie yawned and said goodbye, leaving Willow alone with her thoughts.

Willow crept beneath the light bedspread knowing Clover's body heat would provide an extra covering. She lay awake for a long time, thinking about Martha and Clarissa, as well as Huxley Rune. He had some bad characteristics that was for sure. Stealing Vick's manuscript wasn't the nicest thing to do. But he also had a softer side. Taking care of Clarissa was probably his motive for the theft, especially seeing as how his agent had said he'd been having a dry spell in his writing.

She couldn't sleep so she opened her laptop and did a search of the Reed Rehabilitation Center taking care of Clarissa, as well as the couple running it. She spent hours searching until she fell into a fitful state of sleep. She dreamed of masked murderers and girls in wheelchairs. She kept hearing the beeping of the machine hooked up to Martha. It wouldn't quit. No matter what she did. Finally, she woke and realized it was her phone. The bird was chirping over and over. She must have fallen asleep without turning the sound off.

She dialed Steve's number. He answered on the first ring.

"Are you sitting down?"

"Nope, I'm laying down."

"Oh, well, that works. Guess who is second in line as trustee?"

"Hmm, well, that would be Mark or Elizabeth Reed from the rehabilitation center."

"How did you know?"

"I spent hours looking up financial records, personal records, really anything I could get my hands on. Google is awesome. Well, I also paid for one of those extensive back ground searches. That helped too."

"I think we need to pay our neighbors to the south a little visit. You ready to go?" He paused. "How in the world did you get to be my sidekick anyway?"

"Perhaps it's because I'm pretty good at this." She was pulling on her jeans as she talked. "How far out are you?"

"A country block away."

"Gotta hang up now."

She threw her phone on the bed, let Clover out and ran a toothbrush over her teeth. "Sheesh, I gotta stop staying up all night. I miss too much."

She brought Clover in and had her hairbrush in hand when he pulled in the driveway. She met him halfway. "Can we stop in for a cup of coffee? Please?"

"You read my mind."

She brushed her hair as they drove.

"You really were still in bed, weren't you?"

"You didn't believe me?"

No, I guess I did believe you." He glanced at his watch. "You do know it's after 11, right?"

"I know. I told you I was up late looking these people up. You did hear that part, right?" She emphasized the word right, just like he did.

He pulled into a gas station and got them both a large cup of coffee and a couple of muffins. "I know this isn't as good as yours, but it'll have to do."

"Thank you. It works." She took a sip of her coffee and closed her eyes. "It really is terrible." She started laughing. "But, I'll drink it anyway."

Two hours later they were knocking on the door of the rehabilitation center. The woman who had brought the tray on their first visit opened the door, her eyes wide with apparent fear.

"Can I help you?"

She was trying to send a message with her eyes but Willow was having a hard time understanding it.

Steve responded. "We're here to see Mark and Elizabeth. Are they home?"

Elizabeth chose that moment to further open the door. "Police Chief Grice and Willow, right? Please, do come in. What brings you back our way? I would think you'd have your hands full with murder and the attempted murder on Martha. I'm surprised you took such a long trip with so much going on."

She turned her back and walked toward the same room they had sat in previously. "Can I get you something? Coffee perhaps?"

Steve answered for both of them while Willow, being her normal nosy self, wandered down a hallway. "No. I do have to ask, how did you know there was an attempt on Martha's life? That information wasn't released to the public."

"I'm sure Martha must have called me. We are close, you know. Our mutual concern for Clarissa's wellbeing is such a strong bonding factor."

He laid his hand on the gun at his side. "I don't think so, Elizabeth. I spoke with Martha this morning. She said she hadn't said a word to anyone. Not even you." He continued. "She also remembered what was familiar about the man who tried to kill her in the hospital. What type of cologne does your husband wear? And by the way, where is he?"

Her eyes gave him away when she looked over Steve's shoulder.

Steve quickly turned around to see Mark holding a knife to the maid's throat. Steve trained his gun on the man's forehead. "Put the knife down. You don't want to make this worse than it already is."

[139]

Steve tried to see Willow out of his peripheral vision but couldn't find her. He hoped she was out of harm's way. Knowing Willow though, she was smack dab in the middle of it. He just didn't know how she would play into it, but play into it she would.

Elizabeth had gone to stand next to her husband. It was at that moment she realized Willow was missing. She had been so intent on distracting Police Chief Grice, she lost Willow. Her head started to turn, back and forth, looking for the woman who accompanied the chief to the house. She couldn't find her.

A commotion sounded behind the couple loud enough to startle Mark into lowering his knife, just a little. Willow reached out from behind him and zapped him with her Taser. He dropped to the ground in a fit of muscle spasms. Elizabeth went for the knife but Steve called out to her to freeze, thankfully she followed orders and didn't get herself shot. Then again, it probably would have served her right.

***

Willow settled into her recliner. She had gone to the movie rental store and rented the entire nine seasons of Seinfeld in order to

[140]

understand what Jasper had been talking about. A knock at the door caused Clover to bark. She didn't want to move. She yelled, "Come in. It's open."

Steve pet the top of Clover's head. "Hey girl. You being good? Have you dug any holes lately?"

He moved to the living room where Willow was still relaxing.

"Have a seat."

He sat down on the sofa then gave her the details. She had elected to head straight home and not stay for the questioning. Not that she could have participated. There had to be some rules they followed.

"Well, looks like you were right. Mark and Elizabeth devised a well concocted plan to blackmail Rune. They kept their identity anonymous to make sure they stayed within his good graces. They got used to the money and got greedy. When he had a copy of his will delivered to them, they realized they would be living the high life if he and Martha were out of the way. Clarissa would never be able to report them in her condition so they decided to go for it. They stole Mrs. Frost's laundry and used her yellow housecoat and a wig to lure Rune behind the building. Which, by the way, is what Clyde saw.

They hit him over the head, drug him into the freezer, and fed the lock through the tabs, and basically froze him to death. They knew about Vick and his missing manuscript so they took the one in Rune's briefcase to throw us off. I guess Mark has some lock picking skills, so it wasn't anything to get the basic lock off the freezer door. When they offered me a copy of the will, they conveniently left out the part about the trustees and who controlled the money. If we had that information, we probably would have figured this thing out a lot sooner."

Willow shook her head. "How can people be so cruel?"

"Something good came out of all of this. Martha is going to be taking care of Clarissa at home. With the money Rune left them, she can afford to hire in round the clock care and have her daughter close by."

He picked up the box of dvds. "Hey, I love Seinfeld. No soup for you!" He stated in a terrible Russian accent.

Willow's face was blank. "Come on, you've got to remember that episode. It's a classic."

She shook her head. "I have never seen an episode of Seinfeld."

"Seriously?"

"Seriously!"

He cocked his head. "Oh, your hair looks much better."

She picked up a handful of popcorn and flung it at him. Clover dove for the small morsels, thankful for the treat.

He smiled. "I almost forgot. I'll be right back." He reappeared with a gift wrapped box. "I have something for you."

She started laughing. "A lettuce keeper. Where did you find one?"

"Oh, don't you worry about it. I have people."

"Clarissa gave it to you, didn't she?"

"You know what? You're too perceptive."

She grinned and started the first episode of Seinfeld.

Willow's Six Week Muffin Mix

- 1 15 ounce package bran flakes
- 1 cup vegetable oil
- 3 cups sugar
- 4 eggs, beaten
- 1 qt. Buttermilk
- 5 cups flour
- 5 teaspoons baking soda
- 2 teaspoons salt
- 4 teaspoons cinnamon
- 1 17 ounce can of fruit cocktail, drained

Mix bran flakes, sugar, flour, cinnamon, salt and soda in large square container. Add beaten eggs, oil, and milk. Mix well. Fold in drained fruit cocktail. Do not use batter until it has bee refrigerated one full day.

Dip out, do not stir, when you are ready to make some muffins. (Stirring will break down the leavening and the muffins won't rise.)

Bake 15-17 minutes at 400 degrees F. Batter keeps, covered in the refrigerator, for 6 weeks.

Willow's Peanut Butter Cookies

- 2 ½ cups flour
- 1 ½ teaspoon baking soda
- 1 teaspoon baking powder
- ½ teaspoon salt
- 2 eggs
- 1 cup shortening
- 1 cup peanut butter
- 1 cup sugar
- 1 cup brown sugar

Mix, roll into balls and mash on a greased cookie sheet. Bake 7-9 minutes until lightly browned at 350 degrees F.

This recipe is Lilly's best friend's Mom's recipe from her days as a Yankee. Thank you, Ruth for such a delicious recipe!

Willow's Corn Chowder

- 1 pound of bacon pieces (cut up bacon or buy already in bits and pieces)
- ¼ cup olive oil
- 3 large onions, chopped
- 4 tablespoons butter
- ½ cup flour
- 1 teaspoon pepper
- ½ teaspoon turmeric
- 12 cups chicken stock
- 5 pounds potatoes, peeled and cubed
- 3 pounds frozen corn
- 2 cups heavy cream
- 1 pound of sharp cheddar cheese, divided

In a large stock pot cook bacon until crisp. Remove bacon and excess bacon grease (leave just enough to cover the bottom of the pot). Add olive oil, butter, and onions to the pot and cook until onions until translucent. About 10 minutes on medium heat.

Stir in flour, pepper, and turmeric and cook for 3 minutes. Add the chicken stock and potatoes. Bring to a boil. Simmer until potatoes are tender. Add frozen corn. Cook five more minutes. Add heavy cream and ½ the cheese. Stir until melted. Serve hot garnished with bacon and shredded cheese.

Please enjoy this excerpt from 'This Little Piggy Wound Up Dead', Book 3 of the Willow Crier Cozy Mystery Series

Willow woke to a crash and sat straight up. The dog was whining and pressed up against her. "Some guard dog you are." She heard the little pings of water hitting her bedroom window. The next rumble of thunder gave her an excellent reason to snuggle deeper down in her covers and keep her eyes closed. She loved sleeping to the sound of rain. In her opinion, there was no better sleeping conditions. She pat the dog's head. "It's just thunder, Clover. Nothing to worry about."

She was in that place, in-between consciousness and dreamland when a silent alarm started ringing in her head. It grew louder and as hard as she tried to shut the alarm off, it wouldn't go away. It was an alarm of concern, of something she was forgetting and needed to address.

Her eyes opened and she left the warmth of her cocoon and stood by her bedroom window. "It's raining. So what?" She asked out loud.

Then it hit her. The BBQ cook off. It was rain or shine.

Clover was whining at her feet. "All right, girl. I'll let you out." She opened the back door and the dog hung out on the patio, looking frightened. "Clover, go on, go potty." Clover just stared at her. "Oh good grief. Are you kidding me?" She ran out into the back yard with the dog. "Now go potty! Why do both of us have to get wet?" Clover did her thing then ran for the door.

Willow toweled both of them off on the patio then made her way inside. Everything had been packed up the night before, well, except her duffle bag. She still had a few things to stuff in there. Now she would need ponchos and a few umbrellas. The show must go on.

"Mom, did you grab the hats I bought?"

"Already got 'em. They're sitting on the counter in the kitchen." Willow popped her head out of the bedroom door with her hat already perched on her head. The pink hats with the three little pig's logo were perfect for their first BBQ cook off. "I'm almost ready. Has Steve shown up yet?"

"He just pulled in. Looks like he has the smoker and the grill in the back of his truck. Should I have him put the coolers in there too?"

"Yeah, that'll work." Willow zipped up her duffle bag and set it by the front door. "I think that's it."

She watched as Steve hoisted the heavy cooler into the back of his truck bed. He had a small pull behind camper hooked up for Willow and Embry to use. He said he would be fine in the bench seat of his truck.

Willow was excited. This was her first real BBQ cook off. It was the real deal. She had all four required meats in the cooler, brisket, butt, ribs, and chicken. She walked out and handed Steve his hat.

"Pink, huh?"

She grinned. "Do you have a problem with that?"

"Of course not." He grinned. "Real men wear pink." He placed the hat on his head. "Do you have more that needs loading?"

"Nope, I think this about does it." She tossed her duffle bag into the back of her Jeep. "Everyone ready?"

The Three Little Pigs caravan pulled into the park just after noon. Willow hopped out of her truck opening an umbrella as she landed then told

Steve she was going to check in and figure out where they were supposed to set up.

She returned with a map and a few minutes later, the three of them were busy getting set up. Getting wet in the process.

Willow looked around the park, totally in her element. The smell of smoking meat was driving her crazy. Her stomach rumbled. She decided to take a quick walk and meet a few of the other participants. She wandered from camp to camp, introducing herself and pointing back toward her own camp, telling people to stop by anytime.

Almost everyone was friendly and welcoming. Some were even helpful, giving tips for her first BBQ competition.

Her feet made squishing sounds with each step she took. Her rain soaked tennis shoes were going to be useless. The only other shoes she brought was a pair of flip flops. She leaned up against a big tree and proceeded to kick them off. Angry voices carried as the rain reduced to a drizzle.

"Bridget, I told you to stop talking to him. You're flirting and I won't have it."

"Dean, you don't own me. There's no ring on this finger."

"Own you? Yeah, I do and you know it. Don't you ever think otherwise."

She heard the unmistakable sound of a slap followed by Bridget angrily saying, "You're such a pig, do you know that?"

She saw the back side of Bridget as she stomped back to her camp. She peeked around the other side of the tree to find Dean still cradling his cheek. He started after her. Neither of them noticed Willow.

When Willow returned to camp, she hung her tennis shoes up to dry inside the camper and slipped on her flip flops. The smoker was ready to roll so she prepared her brisket and butt with her seasonings and secured them in the smoker. "Well, for now, that's that. Anyone want to get a bite to eat? We'll need to take turns babysitting."

Embry yawned. "Why don't you two run and get something. Bring me back a sandwich. I'm going to take a nap so I'll be ready for my shift." She held up her phone. "I'll set my alarm. No worries."

Embry crawled in to the readied camper and left Willow and Steve standing in the rain.

"Well, I guess she has it all figured out.

Steve and Willow sat down under a shelter with plates of pulled pork sandwiches, potato salad, and baked beans.

"This rain is giving me the chills." She zipped up her sweat shirt. A voice coming from the table next to theirs captured her attention.

She lowered her voice and told Steve what she had heard earlier when she was out walking.

"Hey, we aren't going to have any trouble this weekend. Not with our equipment, not with our neighbors, and certainly not with a pig. I am off duty. So are you."

She distractedly nodded in agreement. "Do you think that young man she is talking to is the man Dean warned her off from?"

"You didn't hear a word I said, did you?"

"Yes, I did. I was just wondering is all. I can wonder, can't I?"

Steve shook his head. "No, you are banned from wondering. You cannot wonder until you arrive home Sunday evening."

She grimaced then took a bite of her sandwich.

***

Early the next morning Willow crawled out of her bunk and stretched. She smelled coffee. Someone somewhere already had the stuff brewing. It was still dark out. She listened intently. She heard a few hushed voices, a dog barking, a jet ascending, but she didn't hear the pitter patter of rain. She felt the inside of her shoes. Still damp. She had ten minutes until her turn with the smoker. She had to find a bathroom and coffee. And she had to hurry if she didn't want Embry upset with her. The girl was downright ornery when she was tired. Hunger made things ten times worse.

Willow was nearly on top of Dean's camp when a rather behemoth of a man erupted. "I trusted him to keep this thing going. It was his only job. It's not even hot anymore." He turned on the spotlights he had set up around his very large smoker and gathered enough supplies to hopefully get his smoker up and running again. He opened it just as Willow was close enough to hear a string of expletives pour out of the man's mouth. He slammed it shut and stepped back, as though his eyebrows, nose hairs, and chest hairs had all ignited. His smooth bald head was gleaming in the moonlight.

He began speaking gibberish. Willow stepped closer, trying to understand what the man was saying. He kept pointing to the smoker. His eyes danced back and forth between her and the closed unit. She finally had enough with the foreign tourist act and opened the smoker. She stared for a brief moment. Inside was a man, positioned with all fours bent, up in the air and an apple in his mouth.

"Oh goodness. It's the pig."

Author Bio

Lilly York? (aka Darlene Shortridge, author of Contemporary Christian Fiction) How about Lilly Belle; a mis-plant northerner, living in a southern world. Southern charm is lost among late nights with a two year old granddaughter, heat flashes competing with hell, copious re-runs of Murder She Wrote with Jessica Fletcher catching the bad guy, and a vivid imagination keeping insanity at bay.

In both humor and mystery, Lilly draws inspiration from terrible twos, a 24 year old daughter who questions her sanity, a son who constantly spews bad puns, and a husband who has selective hearing. Though, that's perfectly alright with her, because what can you love more than a good laugh and a family so dysfunctional they almost seem functional?

To stay informed on the whereabouts and goings-on of the Willow Crier Cozy Mystery Characters as well as upcoming releases, recipes and maybe a clue or two, join Lilly's e-mail club by going to…

LillyYork.com

A Yankee's Guide to Southern Phrases

Bless Your Heart: The most back handed kind words spoken in the south. Means, while you're sweet, you're also stupid, you don't quite get it and I feel sorry for you.

Fixin to: About to do something, almost ready, thinking about doing something.

Nervous as a long tail cat in a room full of rockin' chairs: Nervous to the point of being jumpy.

Reckon: So suppose or believe something is true.
Yankee: Anyone originating north of the Mason Dixon line.

Redneck: Polite, blue collar individual who loves hunting, country music, and blue jeans. Add alcohol and anything can happen.
Y'all: You guys

All y'all: More than five people

I could eat the north end of a south-bound polecat: Starving!

Lil' Dogie: A motherless calf, a calf separated from its cow.

Hankering: Craving something

Fair to middlin': Doing okay

Three sheets to the wind: Drunker than a skunk

Passel: A whole bunch